"We're not
I don't think we ever were."

Brent moved closer and his voice held the same velvet warmth as the darkness that enfolded them. "Not from that first moment I saw you, a vision of womanhood at dawn, out in the middle of nowhere. You turned to look at me with those huge, defensive gray eyes and I knew then that if we hadn't met before, we certainly should have done."

"Save your romantic patter for someone who might respond to it," Kate said tightly. Brent's words were making her quiver dangerously inside. "I've heard it all before, and I'm not interested. I just want to be left alone."

"Uptight and a liar to boot, Kate?" Brent whispered. "You might want to be left alone, but you are certainly not uninterested."

CAROL GREGOR is married with two children and works as a journalist. She lists her hobbies as "reading, first and foremost, followed by eating and drinking with friends, gardening and films. I am also a private pilot, but a lapsed one since becoming a mother!"

Books by Carol Gregor

HARLEQUIN PRESENTS
1074—MARRY IN HASTE

HARLEQUIN ROMANCE
2732—LORD OF THE AIR

CAROL GREGOR

the trusting heart

Harlequin Books

TORONTO • NEW YORK • LONDON
AMSTERDAM • PARIS • SYDNEY • HAMBURG
STOCKHOLM • ATHENS • TOKYO • MILAN

Harlequin Presents first edition December 1988
ISBN 0-373-11129-0

Original hardcover edition published in 1988
by Mills & Boon Limited

CHAPTER ONE

A THIN white dawn was breaking outside the window, and exotic bird-songs were beginning to pierce the silence. Kate opened her eyes and took in the unfamiliar room. In the next bed Charlie was sleeping peacfully, the only sign of life a lifting and falling of the sheet as he slept off the exhaustion of yesterday's long journey. It was barely half-past five, but she felt wide awake.

We're here! she thought exultantly. I did it! After all these years I really did do it! The words of triumph rolled around her head.

For a time she lay still, but, too excited to sleep, she swung her long legs down from the bed. Their cases were on the far side of the room and she did not want to wake Charlie by rummaging noisily for her robe, so she caught up the sheet from her bed and wrapped it around her before creeping quietly on to the balcony.

Outside the pure air hit her like wine. She stood at the rail and drank it down, feeling it rinse away the last cobwebs of sleep, while the familiar, forgotten smell of dust and wilderness stirred powerful memories.

'I did it!' she repeated fiercely under her breath, savouring the moment.

Six long years ago, broke and alone, she had vowed to herself she would one day bring her son to see the African wilderness which she had loved so passionately in her own childhood.

When she made that promise Charlie had been only four and she had not had the faintest idea how the were going to survive to the end of the week, let alone afford exotic trips abroad. But the promise had been a solemn pact, a symbolic vow to herself, that no matter what hardships lay ahead she would give him the best, the richest childhood that she could possibly manage.

At times it had come to seem absurd, this dream she harboured. One wretched year she had only managed to put eighty pence into the bank account labelled 'Africa'. But life had taken a turn for the better, and the dream had turned into a reality faster than either of them had dared hope.

Her eyes swept the view below the safari lodge. The rooms were clustered in small units all facing down to a waterhole below. In the weak dawn light one or two buck were delicately picking their way from the bushes to drink at the pool, stopping to scent the air with each cautious footstep. Beyond them the tawny plain of scattered thorn trees was growing lighter as the red rim of the rising sum edged towards the horizon. It held a promise of the day's heat to come, and she lifted her face to feel its blessing.

Life was wonderful, she thought. She was no longer broke, and although she was still alone, she had come to prefer it that way. As she stood there, tall and stately in her sheet, her even profile raised to the sun's rays, she felt strong and serene—and quite simply happier than she had felt for years.

'I *did* it,' she repeated, gripping the rail to contain her glee. 'I damn well did it!'

'Terrific.'

A human voice, startlingly close at hand, made her jump. She spun round. A man was standing on the next-door balcony, watching her.

'Well done!' he went on, in a cheerful drawl. 'Are we allowed to ask what?'

She flushed, embarrassed. Then she smiled. Normally she maintained a frosty manner towards unsolicited overtures of any kind, but today she felt generous towards the whole word.

Yet some habits were too deeply ingrained to abandon. Although she took in the impression of a tall, brown-haired man, dressed in khaki bush-shorts and little else, she was careful to keep her gaze from focusing too closely upon him, or meeting his eyes, and she quickly turned back to the view.

'I got here,' she said.

'That's not difficult. You can't get to anywhere else on this road.' His voice was arresting, measured and sure, and curiously familiar.

'You know I didn't mean that,' she said curtly. She kept her eyes on the view, making it plain she did not want to continue the conversation.

'It's beautiful, isn't it?' the man said, following her gaze. 'We had a cheetah and her cubs coming to drink here last week. Every night for five days. Great excitement. But now Sampara Lodge has returned to its customary quiet and calm. In fact it's so early in the season, I suspect you and I are the only occupants.'

Instantly her face closed warily. She glanced at the man, alert for hidden innuendo in the remark, and met a lively brown gaze which made her breath catch momentarily in her throat.

Whoever he was, she thought, he seemed perfectly at home in this wild setting. His hair was chestnut, lit with tawny lights. He was deeply tanned and his rangy body looked fit and easy.

She looked quickly away, back out over the plains.

'I doubt that,' she said coolly. 'I'm sure I saw lights on in a number of rooms last night when I came out for a breath of air.'

The man grinned, totally unabashed by her obvious frostiness. 'Did you wear your toga then, as well?' He nodded at her sheet. 'It's very fetching. I particularly like the off-the-shoulder effect—only perhaps you ought to know that the lodge caters for every contingency. Hanging on the back of your bathroom door you'll find a very luxurious white towelling robe. It's not as dramatic as the sheet, but it's far more effective at keeping the mosquitoes off.'

'Thank you. I dare say I would have discovered that in my own good time. I'm only wearing this because I didn't want to wake Charlie.'

'Charlie?' She sensed, rather than saw, the man raising an eyebrow. 'Funny, my instincts told me you were a woman alone.'

All her antennae went on red alert, and when she turned her eyes on him her look was like granite.

'Well, your instincts were obviously quite wrong,' she snapped. 'I really wouldn't rely on them for anything important.' And, turning immediately, she went back into her room.

She caught sight of herself as she passed the mirror, and the image stopped her in her tracks. She really did look striking. The sheet, flung so heedlessly about her, had fallen into graceful pleats. It left one creamy shoulder bare and emphasised her tall, slender figure. Her face, too, seemed well suited to the classic drapery. It was a perfect oval, with wide-spaced dark grey eyes, fine, arching brows, a straight nose and wide lips. In the dim and distant past various men had told she had the classic beauty of a Greek sculpture or a Parisian model, but when those things had been said she had not felt beautiful, only young and frightened and confused.

In those days she had longed to be small and blonde, with an uptilted nose and a fragile air about her, so that people would have seen her confusion and longed to protect her and look after her.

Now, though—she regarded herself frankly—she was glad she was like she was. At twenty-eight she had finally grown into her looks, she decided. She wasn't young and fragile, and her height and her features reflected honestly the woman she was.

She put her hands up and swept her chin-length dark bob on to the top of her head, turning this way and that to see the effect. Nice slender neck, she decided, good profile. Perhaps she would start to wear it like that from time to time.

She wasn't interested in attracting admirers—she hoped she had made that perfectly clear to the man on the balcony—but she had the usual female interest in looking her best to face the world.

'Mum, honestly! What are you doing?'

She let her hands drop and turned with a smile. 'I'm trying to look like a Roman empress. How am I doing?' She twirled around in her sheet before sinking on to Charlie's bed. 'Did you sleep all right? Or did the hyenas keep you awake? There was one kicking up a real racket just before dawn.'

His eyes, grey like hers but still bearing the roundness of childhood, widened. 'Real hyenas? Honest?'

'Honest. And I've just spoken to someone who told me there's been a cheetah coming to the waterhole.'

'Wow.' He bounced up in bed. 'Have you been out? Without me?

'No, only on to the balcony. I think we should take it slowly today. We'll have to get our bearings, and the heat will probably knock us out for the first day or two.'

'I want to see everything. Lions, giraffes, elephants——'

She brushed a hand across his tousled hair. 'Don't get too excited. It can be quite hard to see things at this time of year. The grass is still high from the rainy season, and the game can hide itself quite easily. It's better later when everything is burnt and shrivelled up.'

'Why didn't we come later?'

'I couldn't wait,' she told him honestly. 'Once we had the money in the bank I just wanted to get here. I've waited six years for this.'

'Me too,' he shouted, bouncing enthusiastically on the mattress. 'Hey, look, we've got our own bathroom, and our own fan—let's see how it works!'

Exuberantly he jumped off the bed and set the electric fan whirling, before throwing open the bathroom door.

'I'm going outside!' he shouted and pushed open the balcony door. Fleetingly she wondered if the man was still there, but her thoughts centred mainly on Charlie. She longed for him to enjoy the bush as much as she had when she was his age, but realistically she knew he might well be bored or disappointed.

He had been swept along on her excitement— had even saved his Christmas money to buy himself a pair of binoculars—but he was a child of the city, brought up in the crowded streets of London, and she guessed that a trip to Disneyland, or some other man-made attraction, might have appealed to him more.

Well, maybe they could do something like that later. This trip was for her, a congratulations present to herself for simply having survived the last years, and a gesture of faith that their health, and even relative wealth, would continue.

She unwrapped her sheet, showered and put on jeans and a khaki shirt.

'Come on, Charlie,' she called. 'Hurry up. I'm starving.'

There was no reply. She opened the balcony door. Charlie stood immobile, binoculars pressed to his eyes, pyjama trousers at half-mast about his hips.

'Look, Mum, over there!' She followed the line of the binoculars.

'What is it?' Instinctively she whispered.

He handed her the binoculars. 'I don't know,' he said. 'It's something. Sort of small and grey with something sticking up.'

She adjusted the lens with a dexterity which came back to her across the years.

'It's a warthog. And it's got some babies with it. If you look to the left you can see them in that clump of grass. The thing sticking up is its tail.'

'We'll have to get a book,' said Charlie later. 'One that helps you identify all the animals.' Already he had started a list, with the date, place and time of every sighting. 'Warthog and babies', he entered carefully at the top of the first page.

She was thrilled by his enthusiasm, and hoped that it would grow rather than diminish during their holiday safari. The important thing would be to make sure he had a good variety of things to do, she thought, noting a swimming-pool on their way to the centre of the lodge complex. The brochure had also listed a games room, film shows and barbecues, and she hoped there might be some other children here for him to make friends with.

But there seemed to be few other people around when they arrived for breakfast.

'I'm sorry, are we late?' she said with a smile to the waiter.

'No, ma'am. It's very quiet this week. Next week there will be more people. The week after——' He spread his hands. 'No room at the inn!' He roared uproariously and carried on chuckling as he set out a huge array of coffee, fruit juice, toast and rolls, and the most wonderful selection of mangoes, papayas and passion fruit.

She looked around. The lodge restaurant was not a room but a large open-air area, sheltered by a thatched roof, which was supported by the branches of trees which grew up between the tables. Bright-plumed birds swooped low under the roof to snatch at crumbs, and no sooner had their breakfast been set out than chattering baboons appeared on the low wall near their table.

Charlie was entranced. She watched him with affection. In London his breakfast was a snatched bowl of cereal while she put on her make-up and shouted at him to hurry for school. They always had to leave early for her to be in the West End in time for her own job, and although she hated leaving him kicking his heels in the playground there seemed to be no alternative until he was old enough to walk the dangerous streets to school alone.

She sighed as she helped herself to another cup of coffee. Hurry and rush. No, hurry and worry and rush. That was what her normal life consisted of. But this holiday would be different. She would think about nothing except the sights and sounds of the bush, and the joy of being deep in the wilderness, away from all the noise and harassment of city life.

'So that must be Charlie?'

Once again the voice make her jump. She looked up, straight into the same direct brown gaze which had interrupted her thoughts earlier. The man was passing their table. Close up she saw he was taller than she had realised, with the kind of lived-in but regular features that she supposed would be called good-looking. For a second she could have sworn she knew him. Yet at the same time she knew she would have remembered if she had met him before.

'Yes,' she said crisply.

'So I wasn't so far off the mark, after all?'

She found she had to look away. There was something about his presence that unsettled her. Not his good looks, but something more subtle, the easy confidence which he betrayed in every movement, the look which held hers, and a very strange feeling that his eyes were taking in far more than she wanted him—or indeed anyone—to see.

'Brent Nicholson.' He put out a hand. His arm, she noticed, was sinewy and deeply tanned. 'Welcome to Sampara Lodge.'

'Are you the manager?' Her voice was clipped. She was proficient at brushing off unwelcome attentions, but she felt deeply dispirited that she should have to bring her talents into play in this remote spot, and at the very start of her holiday.

He grinned widely. 'Alas, no, much as I would like to spend all my days in such surroundings. And you, I surmise, are newly arrived from England, or some similar northern clime—the porcelain winter pallor gives you away.'

She nodded, stiffly. His eyes, when lit by humour,

had curious tawny flecks dancing in their brown depths, she noticed.

He waited. Charlie turned back from the baboons.

'Careful of those, Charlie. They look cute, but they can give you a vicious nip.' Charlie pulled his arm back hastily. 'You need to be careful in the bush, you know,' he said to them both. 'The animals out here aren't pets, and they aren't used to people either. Down in the game parks in the south of the country, or the Serengeti, they've grown pretty used to tourists. You rarely see a lion without its retinue of tour buses. But up here it's a different story, Mrs——'

'Taylor. Kate Taylor. And it's Ms.'

She hadn't wanted the familiarity of a formal introduction, but he had skilfully outmanoeuvered her.

'Was that Ms or Miss?'

'Whichever you like. It's hardly important.'

He acknowledged that with an incline of his head. 'What made you choose Sampara? It's the best game lodge in Kenya, but not many people know about it outside the country. Usually people from America or Europe take the well-worn route—Treetops and places like that.'

'I did my homework.' Deliberately she bent to slice her mango, then his arrogance prompted her to lift her head and regard him with a steely gaze. 'Oh, and I wanted to see a reticulated giraffe, never having seen one further south, and I'd heard there were some interesting species of smaller buck up here—besides the usual klipspringer and oribi.'

She held his eyes and saw his mind working. Slowly his lips parted into a lazy grin, and his eyes danced. His look made her heart skip, and she had to fight an urge to swallow. The grin became a broad smile.

'I see I could have saved my little lecture on the perils of African wildlife.'

His good humour in the face of her rudeness made her soften a little.

'It was rather patronising,' she said coolly. 'But this is Charlie's first time in Africa. I've given him some warnings, but it won't hurt him to hear that it isn't just his mother fussing.'

'And you know Kenya?'

'No. But I spent quite a lot of time in Africa when I was younger—in Tanzania, Zambia and Botswana, and what was then Rhodesia. I would have liked to show Charlie some of those places, but Kenya is cheaper.'

'Not cheap enough, at least for Mike's benefit—he, incidentally, *is* the manager round here.' He swept an arm around the empty tables. 'It's very nice for us that it's so quiet, but it's not so good for profits. He'd rather have full bookings from the very first day of the season.'

'There must be more people here than us.' She sincerely hoped so, otherwise she and this confident stranger would be forced into a proximity which she would not welcome in the slightest.

'A few. I expect they're out on the morning tour. The lodge organises forays into the bush at dusk and dawn. And then you can hire a Land Rover and a guide and set off on your own expedition. I can recommend a couple of days camping on the Lana River, over to the north-west, if you've got the time—there's lion and elephant over there in abundance.'

'Oh, Mum—can we?' Charlie's eyes were eager.

'We'll see. It depends how much it costs.' Her eyes flicked up and caught Brent's gaze, speculative, on her. She could see his thoughts turning, trying to pigeon-hole this single mother with enough cash to come to Africa, but without the limitless funds of many international travellers. She smiled grimly to herself. Well, she wasn't going to make his task any easier for him. She hadn't struggled and fought to shape her own life at home into an impenetrable fortress of domestic peace for her and Charlie, only to have her equilibrium threatened by a chance holiday encounter.

And if Brent Nicholson thought she would be ready prey for his charming grin or quizzically lifted eyebrow, then he had no idea of the fires which had hardened her self-reliance to steel, or the hurts which had given her armour-plated resistance to all advances, however light and diverting they might appear.

Deliberately she hardened her gaze, meeting his look with cold indifference. The brief friendliness she had proffered him was withdrawn. She watched his face stiffen at her look, and he straightened back slowly, pushing his hands down into the pockets of his shorts.

'You can get all the details at the reception desk,' he told her.

'I know.' The words came out like cold pebbles.

His response was his slow, infuriating grin.

'Just trying to be of assistance, ma'am,' he said in a mocking drawl, and he lifted a hand in silent farewell.

His composure in the face of her hostility made her snap in anger.

'We don't need any, thank you. It might be as well if you realised that from the start.' She realised her voice was shaking. Already this man—whoever he was—was spoiling her holiday. 'We got ourselves here by ourselves, and we'll look after ourselves while we're here. Perhaps you should curb your instincts to assist until the next batch of mid-Western matrons comes along! Now if you'll excuse us——' She bit deliberately into her mango, white teeth slicing through the sweet flesh, and turned to watch Charlie set out crumbs of toast for a baby baboon on the veranda wall.

When she turned back, Brent Nicholson was gone and the only remaining breakfasters were the glossy starlings pecking at crumbs by her feet.

CHAPTER TWO

IT HAD been a perfect first day, but now the evening was presenting problems.

Kate had taken Charlie for an early supper and afterwards he had gone happily to bed, exhausted by sun and excitement. But his sleep was light, and every time she moved about the room he muttered and turned in his bed.

She looked at her watch. Only nine o'clock. Although she felt pleasantly relaxed she had no desire for such an early night. She had planned on having a bath and sorting out her clothes, but this was obviously impossible.

After a time she picked up her book and left the room. Charlie would be quite safe. The lodge and all its grounds were patrolled regularly by rangers, and the bar was only a few minutes' walk away.

It was a relief to be able to move freely again, after creeping silently about the room, and she strode thankfully along the sandy path that led to the central complex of the sprawling lodge.

The bar was quiet and she took her vodka and tonic out to the balcony where the only occupants were an elderly couple who smiled with vague friendliness as she took a seat at a corner table.

She looked about, enjoying the surroundings. The

weathered cane tables and chairs looked comfortable and unpretentious against the whitewashed walls and polished red floor. Small geckoes chased flies up the walls in the flickering light from large globe oil-lamps set on the tables. The old-fashioned light was as soft and soothing as the quiet hum of cicadas coming up out of the velvet darkness.

When she caught the couple's glances again the woman signalled quietly to the far corner of the low veranda wall. 'Bush babies,' she mouthed to Kate. 'Watch and see.'

She put her book down silently and waited. On the wall was a large saucer of food scraps, put down as if for a pet cat or dog. Above it was a dark mesh of branches. As she looked, eyes straining into the blackness, there was a scurry of movement and a small furry animal jumped down to the food. It scooped some into its paws, turned huge headlamp eyes towards its human audience and then scampered quickly away.

She exchanged a smile with the couple. Out in the distant bush there was the short distinctive cough of a hunting lion, and shortly afterwards the bray of a hyena. A shiver a delight went through her. This was what she had come for, she thought, the sights and sounds and smells of Africa which she had missed so badly.

'Well, hello. Watching our furry babies?'

It was that voice again. Automatically her knuckles tensed around her glass. Brent Nicholson appeared from the bar, a beer in his hand, and strolled towards her table. He took a swallow, raised a hand to the couple, and showed no sign of moving on.

'Can I get you something? A refill?' He nodded at her glass

'No. Thank you.'

She raised her book ostentatiously and began to read, but the print danced and jumped before her eyes. She put up a poor pretence of concentration, and she knew he could see it.

'You'll strain your eyes trying to read in this light,' he observed unhelpfully. 'And it's far too beautiful a night to bury your nose in a book. Look at that moon.'

She followed his pointing hand. It hung like a large silver coin in a navy sky, flooding the bush beneath with a pale, translucent light. She could have watched it for hours, but not in the presence of Brent Nicholson.

'May I?' He was already pulling back a chair and settling at her table.

She opened her mouth, then closed it again. 'I——' What could she possibly say? 'I wish to be alone'? 'I want to read my book'? Perhaps he would drink down his beer and go.

'Your boy's a pretty keen bird-watcher,' he said, apparently oblivious of her ill-humour. 'I saw him out by the pool this afternoon, with the binoculars and notebook.'

'Yes.'

'How old is he? Eleven or thereabouts?'

'Ten.'

He scrutinised her face. 'You don't look old enough to have a son of that age—it's corny, but it's true.'

'Well, I am. And I do.' She felt anger fermenting inside her. 'Look, Mr Nicholson——'

'Brent. Please.'

The name stuck in her throat. 'Look——' She moved forward in her chair. He put up a hand.

'I know. You're still mad about this morning. I'm sorry I offended you. I didn't mean to patronise you and I apologise. There. Now can we forget it?'

His impudence astounded her. He seemed to have no awareness at all that his presence was unwelcome. 'I don't give a damn about this morning,' she said through clenched teeth, and suddenly the words were coming out in a furious, fluent stream. 'What I do care about is that you understand from the first that I'm here for a quiet holiday with my son. If I'd wanted it any other way then I'd have chosen a more appropriate place to be—oh, I don't know, chatted up, or picked up, or "to form interesting new relationships", or whatever words you want to dress it up in! Just because I'm here without a man doesn't mean I'm automatically in the market for a replacement partner! It's a mistake that I've grown very tired of in London, and I haven't come all these thousands of miles to have to confront it all over again! I'm sorry to be so blunt, but I've only got a handful of days here, and they are very, very precious to me. I don't intend to waste a single, solitary one of them on mistakes or misunderstandings with fellow guests!'

She flung back in the chair and the cane creaked in urgent protest. Her eyes, when angry, grew dark and large, and colour flushed to her cheeks. Her lips were pressed angrily together, and she tossed her hair back as she raised her chin to confront his look.

He watched her in silence for a moment, taking in her anger. Then he leant forward. There were smile creases at the corners of his eyes, but his response was swift and cutting.

'Well, perhaps I should tell *you* something, Kate Taylor. I don't know what terrible trials you've had to put up with in London. I can see it must be most tiresome having to wade through those throngs of suitors every day. But out here in Africa we retain some of the common decencies of life. I'm sorry if you consider the simple desire to exchange a friendly remark or two with an acquaintance the equivalent of rape and assault, but I would suggest you are going to find it hard to get through your time here without handing out a word here and there!'

'That's not what I meant, and you know it!'

'All I know is that I passed an observation on your youthful looks and you chose to interpret it as a wish to drag you into the bushes by your hair and do evil to you!'

His eyes wrinkled with cool humour, but his voice was harsh. In its anger she heard a South African twang creep into his vowels, and an objective part of her mind logged that he must have been born and bred on this wild continent.

She flushed and lifted her head high to carry off her anger. The soft lamplight showed her skin at its best and lit the slender haughtiness of her throat.

'You're deliberately misinterpreting me! You know I what I mean. I came out here for a peaceful drink. I wasn't looking for company.'

'You could have said so,' he cut in. 'I would have happily joined Mr and Mrs Powell.'

'Perhaps I'm too polite to! Perhaps I'm the one with the "common decency" you're so quick to claim! Most people would have had the sensitivity to realise they weren't exactly welcome at this table, but you chose to ignore the fact—that's what I'm talking about. I'm afraid I've met far too many men whose arrogance makes them believe their advances are always welcome, their company a priceless gift—and I'm just not willing to go through all the tedious rituals that that entails any more. So please let's get things straight right from the start.'

She closed her book tightly and sat forward, her wrists crossed on top of it, her eyes challenging his coldly. His met her look levelly. His face had finally lost its good humour and its lean planes were set.

He tapped a finger to his brow. 'Message received and understood—although I'll leave you with this thought.' He levered his long legs up from the low chair and towered over her seated figure, his eyes holding hers. 'If we're talking of arrogance perhaps you'd better consider just how much arrogance there is in assuming that every male for miles has nothing on his mind but wanting to get you into bed. It's insulting to men and breathtakingly presumptuous about the power of your own attractions. Goodnight.'

Casually he threaded his way between the tables. As he drew near the elderly couple they looked up, greeting him with wide smiles, and soon all three were in animated conversation. She wanted to run away, into the darkness, but she forced herself to finish her drink slowly, her book open on her lap although the words were jumbled nonsense. When she got up to leave, she noticed that Brent did not even glance round.

Damn the man! she thought fiercely as she walked back to her room, and, again, intermittently throughout the night as the unaccustomed night noises woke her from a troubled sleep and his caustic words came back to embarrass and anger her.

It was a great relief when dawn was heralded and she could shake Charlie awake and urge him to hurry for the morning game-viewing trip. This left before first light for a drive around the game park, and stopped for an outdoor breakfast before returning to base as the mid-morning sun drove the animals to find shade.

They thought they were late as they ran up to the Land Rover waiting at the gate, but the vehicle was empty apart from the driver slouched at the wheel, a bush hat tipped over his eyes.

'I'm sorry if we've kept you waiting——'

The driver levered himself up in the seat and the hat tipped back.

'That's OK, ma'am.'

'You! Oh, no!'

Her discomposure caused Brent obvious amusement. 'I'm afraid I'm all that's on offer today. Doug Anderson, who usually does these trips, is laid up with a leg ulcer, and Mike has had to rush off to Nairobi, so I've had to step into the breach.' His eyes mocked her. 'Don't worry, I know the difference between an elephant and an egret. I even know where you're most likely to spot some of those reticulated giraffe you're so keen to see. But of course if you don't feel safe with me——'

'Oh, Mum.' Charlie didn't understand the conversation, but he sensed from the atmosphere that the trip might be in doubt.

'It's all right. Get in. There's no problem.'

Kate felt angry and thrown. All her instinctive fears that this man could spoil her longed-for holiday now seemed justified. And she felt completely at sea with him. She had taken him for a guest, but it seemed he actually worked here, which made everything three times as difficult——

She climbed up behind Charlie, into the seat directly behind Brent, with a frown on her face. Almost immediately he started the engine.

'Shouldn't you wait? There may be other people coming.'

'We're already fifteen minutes late. If we leave it any longer the sun will be up before we've got anywhere, and you'll be lucky to see more than a few Tommies.'

'What are they?' Charlie chipped in. He was on the edge of his seat with excitement at the prospect of his first trip into the bush. Brent laughed.

'Thomson's gazelles. They're a small kind of buck—deer, you'd call them in England. They're pretty little fellows, brown with a black stripe down the side, but they're as common as can be. You see hundreds of them, all over the place.' He half turned in his seat. 'Why don't you come up front with me,

Charlie? You'll get a far better view.'

Charlie needed no further bidding, and scrambled over the seat with alacrity. Brent screwed round further in his seat and cocked an eyebrow at Kate. There was wickedness in those brown eyes, she thought, and she felt an uncomfortable worm of apprehension wriggle in her stomach. If he chose to exact revenge for her harsh repulsion of him last night then she could see she might well have met her match.

'How about you, Kate?' He indicated the seat next to him. 'There's room for three up here.'

Nervousness made her curter than she intended. 'I'm quite comfortable here.'

He grinned at her sardonically. 'Oh well, it's your nose you're cutting off. Let's go.'

For the first mile or so they drove across an open brown plain.

'You won't see much here,' Brent told them, 'there's too much traffic. This is the road to the airstrip and the village where the lodge workers live.'

Her gaze shifted from the landscape, pale and grey in the first light of dawn, to the outline of Brent in front of her.

She had thought him rangy, but she could see now that his shoulders were broad and strong. She could see the slight waywardness of his thick hair, its bends and waves of dark chestnut turned to black by the thin morning light, and she could see the casual way his hands guided the wheel of the vehicle along the rough track, confident and experienced.

Beside him Charlie's outline was thin-necked and boyish, absurdly topped by the wide-brimmed hat Brent had playfully transferred from his own head.

She looked away. What was it about him? she thought. Not just that he was a powerfully attractive man. She had seen that at first glance and it was irrelevant to her. There wasn't a man in the whole world handsome enough to break through the steel armour she had encased around her responses to the opposite sex.

No, it was something far less obvious. He had presence, she thought, remembering a favourite phrase of her mother's. She could see that wherever he was, in whatever company, he was the one who led the way, called the tune. He was charming, easy, deeply confident—and totally unused to being spurned or ignored.

l, she resolved, he would have to get used to it, at least as far as she was concerned. Because she simply wasn't interested in any man, and her indifference was the powerful weapon with which she would fight his insidious attraction.

She looked away, out of the window. The sky was lightening to gold in the east and colour was beginning to tinge the grasses and the trees. They turned off the wide dirt road on to a narrow track which wound across the open grassland to a line of trees.

'Palms,' said Brent. 'Elephant love them.' The denser undergrowth cast shadows into the Land Rover and there was a scent of water on the air. Suddenly Brent slowed right down and pointed.

'What! Where?' Charlie knelt up.

'Shhh.' Brent guided his gaze to a dark mass among the trees. Kate looked. The mass turned its head and she could see at once it was a large bull buffalo browsing peacefully.

'Is it an elephant?' Charlie hissed.

Brent shook his head, and explained.

'Buffalo,' he said, turning back to look at Kate.

She nodded, not taking her eyes from the animal. 'I know'

After a moment it lifted his head, heavy with curving horns, and stared towards them. Charlie looked nervous.

'Don't worry,' she told him quietly. 'We're quite safe.'

After a few moments they drove on and as they came out of the trees they began to see herds of buck and one or two zebra. Then Charlie spotted a warthog trotting through the grass and they stopped to watch its bustling progress.

All this time the sun was rising, taking the chill from the air and turning the world to a dramatic red and then gold. They all peeled off sweaters and Kate wound down the window to let the bird-song flood in, as crystal clear as the morning air. They could hear the peaceful grunts and snorts of the browsing game and a rising hum of insects.

The sky was huge, a vast vault of perfect blue arching over a scene of such peace and harmony that she quite forgot anything except the deepest pleasure of the moment.

She rested her arms on the edge of the window, sank her chin down and feasted her gaze.

'We'll drive on to the waterhole beyond that little ridge, and watch for a while,' Brent said. 'Then we'll think about breakfast.'

'Will we see any lions?' asked Charlie.

'You might,' Brent said. 'But you have to be patient. You can't summon any animals to order. You just have to wait and see what comes your way.'

Kate smiled. It would be difficult for him, she knew. Charlie was a child of the city, and of the electronic age, who believed everything was instantly available, if you just knew where to get it, or had the cash to buy it with.

That had been one reason for coming to Africa—to show him a world that was the opposite of the hustle and bustle that made up his daily life. But not the main one. That had been for herself, and herself alone. To nourish herself on the sights and sounds that had so enriched her girlhood, and to try and find again something of the peace she had known before everything had gone so horridly wrong.

The waterhole was a perfect spot for watching game. They sat in near silence watching the antics of a troop of baboons, and the delicate comings and goings of the buck. Then Brent lifted a pair of binoculars and studied some dark shapes moving towards them. He touched Charlie's arm and told him to do the same. Kate watched him struggle, rather ineptly, to focus the glasses. When he finally managed to his face split into a watermelon grin. 'Elephant!' he said. 'Oh, and they've got babies. Look, Mum.'

Kate took the glasses and ranged them over the

scene until she found the family heading purposefully towards the waterhole.

'Two cows, two young ones and a baby,' Brent pronounced. He turned to Charlie. 'They're the most intelligent animals there are. You ask any tracker or ranger what his favourite animal is and he'll tell you the elephant. They're sensible, loving, gentle—unless roused by pain or fear—and loyal. Far better than we humans, in fact.' He turned to look at Kate. 'Wouldn't you say?'

She met his eyes and looked away.

'Absolutely,' she said with cold deliberation, and her voice was so imbued with old pain that he looked curiously at her until she felt forced to divert his gaze.

'What's that eagle?'

She pointed to the huge bird of prey hovering above them.

'I'm not sure. It's a bit too high to see. It's probably a brown eagle, or maybe a fish eagle. A few hunt along the river over there. We'll just wait for the elephant to arrive, and then we'd better think about breakfast.'

Charlie looked disappointed, but Brent tempted his hungry stomach with talk of ham and egg rolls. 'There's nothing like a dawn start for making you ravenous by nine o'clock.'

Kate checked her watch. Ten to nine. On a normal day she would be waving goodbye to Charlie at the school gate and rushing towards the tube, already tense and anxious about the day ahead. This morning the only tension she felt was the uneasiness which lay between her and Brent, and that was the merest pinprick of discomfort when set against the glorious fact of simply being here, out in the wilds of Africa.

She sighed.

'Bored?' Brent turned to look at her and, meeting his eyes afresh, she again had the elusive, fleeting feeling that she had known him somewhere before. She dismissed it instantly.

'Never less so. Look, they've finally got here.'

Through the spindly scrub came the stately grey elephant, trunks swinging towards the scent of water. One of the mothers gently nudged her baby towards the water's edge, and Kate laughed at the familiar gesture. 'It's like me trying to get you washed before school, Charlie.' The boy grinned, then laughed out loud as one of the young beasts lumbered down into the shallows and began to blow water over its back.

'The morning shower,' said Brent, and he reached forward to switch on the engine. Then he turned to her. 'Look,' he said, 'it's a rocky ride from here on. You'll be bouncing about like a pea on your own in the back. You'd be better off in the front.'

She hesitated. He smiled sardonically. 'Don't worry, I've got no designs on you—especially after that friendly little outburst last night. Quite frankly, one denimed thigh is much like another when this thing is shaking about like a bucking bronco and everyone's being hurled here and there. And anyway I'll need to keep both hands firmly on the wheel.'

Her eyes flicked instantly to Charlie and she scowled at Brent, but the boy was still absorbed by the elephant antics. Suddenly he pointed, shouting excitedly, 'Look, look!'

Brent whipped round. The animals at the water's edge were sniffing the air, tensed and poised. Charlie had spotted a slink of tawny fur. Following the boy's pointing arm, Brent said at once, 'Lion.' He watched for a moment. 'It's a female, a large one. Look, she's already singled out her prey. She's after that young buck there.' As they watched the lion squirmed and stalked the vulnerable animal, separating it gradually from the rest of the group until she crouched back on her haunches and made the final spring, so fast that all they could see was a blur of fur and dust and the thin sticks of the buck's legs upended in the air.

The other animals at the waterhole spread in a panicked confusion, coughing and grunting in alarm, all except the elephant who took no notice of the drama being enacted beneath their giant feet.

They watched transfixed as the sad twitchings of the prey finally stopped and the lion, standing over it, raised her head and sniffed the air before beginning to drag the carcass towards a clump of thorn scrub.

Brent pointed at the trees. 'The vultures are already gathering. There'll be dozens here within minutes.' Again he turned to look at Kate, and she saw an assessing look in his brown eyes. 'They'll be dipping their heads into the carcass until they turn as red as turkeys. And you should see the short work those beaks and talons can make of even the largest intestines.'

She smiled to herself. He wanted her to shudder, to show some evidence of feeble feminine distress at such savagery.

'I have,' she said. 'It's not a pretty sight, but it's efficient. There's no waste and everyone gets fed.'

He smiled. 'You have to admit it's savage, though. That was a nice, clean kill, but I've seen a pack of wild dogs tear a young zebra limb from limb—while it was still alive. And once——'

'Look,' she cut him off angrily, 'I dare say you like to think we're a couple of ignorant tourists who believe the animals are as cuddly as in a cartoon strip, but I've seen enough on my travels to know better, and I've told Charlie what to expect. We really don't need your horror stories for our education.'

He was doing it to provoke her, she knew, but Charlie was just a boy. Although she knew he had a robust constitution and could easily stomach the sight he had just watched amd more, Brent didn't. For all he knew, his lurid tales could well result in childhood nightmares.

She glanced across at Charlie, and Brent, seeing her look and realising what it implied, had the grace to look abashed.

'Yes, I'm sorry. I forgot you were an old Africa hand. I've seen so many visitors who think lions are gorgeous pussycats, and hippos are cute little bath toys, that my commentary tends towards the abrasive. Now hop in the front and we'll get going.'

There seemed to be no reason to resist his

command, although she began to regret it on the journey. The violent lurching of the vehicle constantly threw her against Brent, and although he seemed quite impervious, she was acutely aware of the warmth of his shoulder and the hardness of his thigh. To save herself, she put an arm behind Charlie's seat and braced herself firmly from the worst of the joltings, but she guessed Brent noticed her discomfort because an unsettling private smile seemed to play about his etched lips.

'What took you travelling to Africa?' he asked as they sat by a small camp-fire polishing off a copious breakfast. Kate thought she had never had coffee so delicious as that brewed on the flames, or rolls that were so fresh. Her plate was clean and she was now attacking an apple. Brent, who had lit the fire, made the coffee and laid out the breakfast with all the proficiency of a Savoy chef, had complimented her on her healthy appetite, remarking he couldn't stand finicky women who lived on kiwi fruit and mineral water.

'My father. He was an engineer in Rhodesia and later in Zambia.' She smiled. 'Not a very successful one. He preferred travelling to working. Really he should have been an explorer, or maybe a district commissioner in the days of the Empire. He and my mother were divorced, and I lived with my mother in England, but every summer I used to go out and spend a month with Dad, and we always went off on some expedition or other.'

If she closed her eyes she could still recall the thick smell of his old canvas tent, and the fumes from the ancient lamp that they lit as darkness fell.

Brent reached for an apple. 'Where did you go? To the Luangwa Valley?'

'Yes. Twice.'

'And Chobe?'

'Yes.'

'And Kariba?'

'Yes.'

'So you've been around.' He was sitting cross-legged on the sand, looking at her over the rim of his coffee-mug, and his eyes danced with mocking lights.

She swallowed and made her gaze grey and cold. 'I hardly think that's the way to put it.'

'Around Africa, I mean.'

'I know what you mean.'

The sharp exchange crackled in the air. Charlie got up and walked away. Brent glanced round. 'Don't go too far,' he warned.

'He knows that. He's very sensible.'

'I dare say, but it's my job to tell him. You're both my responsibility until you're safely back at the lodge.'

'Then maybe we should get going——' She did not want to leave. It was so peaceful sitting where they were on a little hill of boulders overlooking the golden plains beneath. The air was freshened by a morning breeze which stirred the thick swing of hair about her shoulders, and barely a sound disturbed the deep silence. But Brent seemed determined to goad and hound her, and she had no intention of remaining a sitting target.

'You'd find it all changed now. There's tarmac roads and luxury lodges everywhere, and sightseers by the bus-load.'

'I don't know—here it all seems just as I remember Africa to have been.'

'Oh, no, you wait till the season gets under way. Any poor lion that shows his nose is immediately dogged by at least one dormobile. And the ignorance!' He raised his eyes to heaven. 'Do you know, a man once asked me whether bat-eared foxes could fly!'

She laughed, but reluctantly. 'You don't seem to have a very high opinion of your clients.'

'Clients.' He was puzzled. 'Oh, the tourists, you mean. No, I don't. To be honest, I wish they'd all go back to America or Japan or Sweden, or wherever it is they came from.'

'You ought to feel sorry for us, not contemptuous,' she said tartly. 'We don't all have the chance to live in places like this.'

'I ought,' he agreed smoothly, 'but I don't. You may have gathered that patience and tolerance are not among my many virtues. Some people don't suffer fools gladly—I don't suffer them at all.'

His remarks were pointed, aimed, she knew, at her rebuttal of him the night before. Her eyes locked to his in antagonism, but he sat surveying her with equanimity, a taunting half-smile playing about his lips. He had a very attractive mouth, she noticed irrelevantly, firm and pleasant, with teeth that showed white against his tan. She felt something catch in her stomach and her fingers tightened in her palms.

'And you may not have gathered,' she said tensely, 'that I'm not remotely interested in your virtues or lack of them. I'm here to enjoy the animals—the four legged variety, that is—and I don't intend to let anyone get in the way of that.'

He looked at her for a long moment, and when he spoke his voice was deep and deliberate. 'May I be so bold, Ms Taylor, as to suggest that the only person likely to stop you enjoying your holiday is yourself. You're as wound up as spring——'

'Stop it!' She jumped up and began to walk away. 'Whatever you've got to say, I don't want to hear it!'

'Where are you going?'

'For a walk.'

He grinned that infuriating smile. 'Well, watch out for snakes. They like to bask on these sunny rocks.'

She looked round at him with contempt. If he intended to frighten her he wouldn't succeed. She had taken snakes in her stride before, not even panicking when a puff adder had chosen to curl itself against the warmth of her sleeping-bag one cold night in the wilds of Zambia.

Silhouetted against the sky she looked tall and slender, strong and aloof. Brent squinted against the sun to take in the sight of her.

'Don't be long,' he admonished.

She did not deign to reply but strode purposefully out of sight.

When she returned Charlie was nowhere to be seen.

'Where's Charlie?'

'He wanted to walk down to the plain and I said we would pick him up on the way.'

'But——'

'He's quite safe. Any animals lurking in these rocks would have been frightened off by our picnic. And anyway, I've got him covered.' He lifted a hand casually to show her the rifle he was holding. 'I don't believe in leaving myself unprotected—in that, at least, we've got something in common.'

'What do you mean?'

'I mean you protect yourself with harsh words. I protect myself with a gun. Badly used, they can both have the same effect, as well.'

She looked at him, eyes wide. He made her nervous, this arrogant, confident stranger, who seemed entirely unperturbed by her habitual frostiness. She was never sure what he would say next.

For a moment he said nothing. Then he deliberately stepped closer to her, leaning an elbow against the side of the Land Rover. She saw the thin khaki cotton of his shirt stretching over firm muscles, the tautness of his thighs in the battered blue jeans. He looked at one with the landscape, she thought, his face lean and tanned, tawny lights in his hair and his brown eyes flecked with gold. He was a lion of a man, she realised suddenly, arrogant and calmly certain of his authority. He made her quail inside. Worse, he was beginning to make her body stir with a beat of heat that she did not want or welcome. But she would show him nothing of this.

She raised her head and met his eyes, almost on a level.

'In both cases they can have the opposite effect to that intended,' he said. 'A bad shot can prompt an animal to spring, and defensive words can prompt exactly the kind of pursuit they are intended to deter.'

She met his look bravely, helped by the anger that spurted inside her. 'I've told you, I'm not on the market, not in any way. I don't know what game you're playing with me, but I want no part of it! All I want to do is enjoy this holiday which I've saved so hard for and I've no intention of letting any jumped-up safari guide who doesn't seem to know his place stopping me——'

'And what about Charlie?' he put in.

'What do you mean?' She was thrown. Her eyes searched his.

'I mean that unless you unwind a bit, unclench those fists of yours—unclench your mind—you'll be about as good company for him and anyone else as one of those prickly euphorbias down there.'

His words bit home. She rejected them with all the mental force she could muster.

'Why don't you stop interfering in things you know nothing about!' she shouted. 'My relationship with my son is nothing to do with you.'

'So why do you think he's gone off now? I'll tell you why. Because he didn't feel comfortable here——'

'And who's fault was that? You've been trying to

provoke me all morning!'

'Nonsense. A bit of harmless teasing, maybe——'

'And maybe not!' Her voice was high and sharp with anger. 'If you're so worried about Charlie, Brent Nicholson, I'll tell you what you can do about him. You can leave both him and me alone!'

His eyes stripped across her. He was not smiling now. He took in her proud figure and combative grey gaze, before going insolently down over her lips, her neck, her figure.

'Perhaps I'd like to,' he said shortly. 'Unfortunately, under these particular circumstances, it's the one thing that simply isn't possible.'

CHAPTER THREE

IT WAS evening. Kate had walked away from the lodge and was sitting by herself on a tree-stump watching the sunset.

It had been beautiful at first, a ripe and mellow light flooding the landscape, but now it was turning into a spectacle that was both magnificent and melancholy. Vivid ribbons of pink and purple cloud lay across the sun, which was a blood-red ball dropping rapidly from sight. As it did so the landscape darkened and the bush grew silent.

She remembered, now, that this had always happened. As the light went from the sky the bush became as silent and still as the grave. Nothing moved, nothing made a noise. For an hour or more, sometimes, there would be no sound, and then the hidden life of the night would get under way with the first occasional grunts and howls from the night creatures.

She used to love that mysterious pause, sitting by the campfire with her father waiting for the first hyena to laugh or jackal to howl, but tonight the sinister sunset chilled her to the bone.

She felt lonely and sad, acutely aware of life slipping fast through her fingers before she had a chance to hold and relish it.

She shivered and drew her knees up to her chin, hugging them round with her hands. It wasn't cold, but she felt chilled by unhappy thoughts.

Perhaps, she thought, it was inevitable that she should feel this way. Coming back to Africa had roused a million memories of her father, and although they were happy recollections, from the days when everything had still been fine, she could never now think of him without pain.

She examined this thought and rejected it. It was more than those old, buried wounds that was making her feel this way. It was Brent Nicholson, she thought savagely, with the impertinence of his mockery and unsolicited criticisms.

What right had he to say the things he had said this morning? No one had spoken to her like that for years. At work no colleague would dare to venture such personal remarks, and her friends respected her self-containment—that was exactly why they were her friends. As for men, well, no man had been allowed to become close to her for years.

That was how she wanted to live her life, and she had worked hard to achieve this privacy.

But Brent Nicholson had simply barged in with his homespun philosophies and blunt truths and set doubts and uncertainties seething wildly around her brain.

Uptight, he had called her, as wound-up as a spring. She looked down at her hands curled tight about her legs. The trouble was, there was an element of truth in what he said. Her life in London, with all the responsibilities of looking after Charlie and holding down her job, had come to seem a very serious business. She felt that if she let go for a moment, let her guard slip, then all its careful construction would slide into chaos.

Slowly, deliberately, she unclenched each finger, stretching and relaxing them. It felt unusual, and she had to admit it felt good. She sighed deeply and felt the muscles along her jaw release as well.

Unclench your mind, he had said, and he was probably right. She could see all too clearly how he saw her—a defensive, aggressive woman, unable to take a joke or manage the simplest bit of repartee, and perhaps that was true. She had grown strained, stilted, maybe even humourless. Last night's outburst had been a ridiculous over-reaction—she should have handled his unwelcome attentions with far more grace—and this morning, in his company, she had been as jumpy as a cat.

She sighed again. Well, she would try to relax a bit more when she next saw him, and treat him with normal friendliness. She might even proffer an apology for her rudeness, and that way hope to lay the whole uncomfortable episode to rest before it soured the remainder of her holiday.

The trouble was, it wouldn't be easy. Brent seemed to see her as a prey to be teased and goaded, as a cat might play with a mouse, and then there was the other thing—no matter how firmly her mind rejected him, her body was beginning to stir over him in a way she found impossible to subdue.

Suddenly restless, she stood up and stretched her stiff muscles. The sun had gone completely now and

night was creeping across the sky from the east. The
blood was pumping through her body again and she
had an urgent desire to push away the night with
light and laughter. She headed towards her room,
and a warm shower, her mind already turning on
the clothes she would wear for supper.

'Mum, you look smashing,' Charlie said when
she emerged from the bathroom. She had bathed
and changed into a white silk shirt and silk trousers
patterned in red and black. She had looped her hair
back behind a broad red band and put on her
enamelled earrings. The effect was exactly what she
wanted. She looked young and beautiful and sexy in
a cheerful sort of way. Her gloom had been washed
away with the water that had swilled off the dust of
the day, and she felt happy once more and ravenous.

'Come on,' she said, swinging an arm about
Charlie's shoulders, 'I could eat a horse.'

'A lion!' Charlie shouted.

'A buffalo!'

'An elephant!'

She had to admit she was disappointed when they
reached the restaurant terrace and she saw that the
tables were deserted and there was no one to see the
striking figure she cut as she made her entrance.

Or was it that she was disappointed Brent was not
there, she asked herself honestly, as she sipped her
drink. Were the clothes and the earrings and the
make-up all just an elaborate declaration to him that
she was not the tight-lipped woman he thought she
was?

The food came and they attacked it with gusto,

talking over the day's events. She eyed Charlie fondly. Already he was exchanging his winter pallor for a tan and his eyes were bright with excitement. She only hoped that he would not get too bored with mere animals and adults to help him while away the days.

'Excuse me, is everything all right?'

She swung round and met a ruddy-faced man, with an open smile, dressed in an immaculately pressed safari suit.

'Yes. Thank you.'

'I'm Mike Mather, the manager. I'm sorry not to have seen you before but we've had one or two problems keeping us busy. You must be Ms Taylor—and Charlie.'

She nodded.

'This is my wife, Sandy. We were just going to eat ourselves.'

Kate smiled at the friendly-looking woman. 'Would you like to join us? Or is it too much like work to eat with the guests—I'd understand if you said yes.'

Mike laughed. 'It's a treat. We get sick of our own company, especially by the end of the closed season.'

'You're one of our earliest guests, Ms Taylor,' said Sandy, sitting down.

'Kate, please. Ms Taylor makes me feel a hundred! I'm glad it's not too crowded. I'm enjoying the quiet, although I don't know about Charlie——'

Mike said, 'Perhaps we can do something about that. We had to drive down to Nairobi today to pick up our boys from school. They've got the plague, or something, sweeping through the place and they've had to close down to try to get it under control.'

'Mike!' Sandy laughed. 'It's only chicken pox, which ours have had anyway.'

'Well, we've brought them back for a bit. They've gone to bed early tonight but you're bound to see and hear them tomorrow. Adam's nine and Joe's twelve. They're not exactly unobtrusive!'

Charlie's face brightened. Kate said, 'That'll be wonderful. Mums aren't much fun on holiday. All they want to do in the hot part of the day is sleep and read!'

'Did you see much game this morning?' Mike asked. 'I'm sorry I wasn't there to do the run myself, but I heard you went out on the ride.'

She flashed him a quick look, wondering just what he had heard, but Charlie launched immediately into an excited account of the lion kill at the waterhole. Both Mike and Sandy were impressed.

'You were lucky to see that,' said Mike.

'It's Brent,' said Sandy. 'That man was born under a lucky star. We never saw a cheetah near the lodge until he arrived. Then we began to see them every night!'

'Was he OK?' Mike asked. 'We aren't getting our full staff here until next week, and have to make do with whoever's around.'

She frowned, puzzled. 'Yes, he was fine. He obviously knows the bush backwards.'

Sandy said, 'He was born in South Africa, but his parents moved north to farm in Rhodesia. I think he worked as a ranger somewhere down south at one time, although that's all rather lost in the mists of time. Anyway he certainly knows his game.'

Kate was even more puzzled.

'But isn't he a game-ranger now?'

'Uh uh.' Mike shook his head. 'Is that what he told you? You mustn't believe a word he says. No, technically he's a guest, albeit a kind of house-guest. He's spent the last couple of months up here writing a book. He's been a foreign correspondent for years—you must have seen him on television. He's covered just about every coup and revolution and civil war there's been in Africa of late.'

'Oh!' Suddenly it all slipped into place. The familiarity of the face, and the voice, that curious feeling she had known him before, coupled with the absolute certainty that she had never met him. At least she had, but only as a figure on the news, speaking urgently of happenings in places that were often just names to her. 'I thought he seemed familiar——'

Mike laughed again. 'Brent says little old ladies come up to him in the street and pat him on the arm and ask him how he's keeping. They think they've known him for years just because they've seen him on the television——'

'And women,' Sandy put in. 'He said he didn't know fame was such an aphrodisiac. Girls he's never met before have offered him their all just because of who he is!'

Kate pressed her lips together. She could imagine that very well. Although was it the fame alone, or the mocking warmth of those brown hunting eyes?

'I thought he seemed familiar,' she repeated, 'but I didn't know why. I'm afraid I never give the news my full attention.'

'Too busy?' Sandy said, sympathetically.

'Yes. I rarely get home before six and by the time we've eaten and wrestled with Charlie's homework the evening seems to have flown.'

'What do you do?' Mike asked.

'It's a bit difficult to explain. I work for one of the big London stores, planning promotions and sales projects. Technically I'm called the development manager, brackets projects, but I do anything from planning Santa's Christmas grotto to thinking up ways of promoting new lines. We've just had a big push on sportswear, and when I get back we'll be looking into whether we should open a personal finance centre in the store.' A vision of the paperwork piled on her desk flashed through her mind and she instinctively tensed her shoulders at the thought of the mounds of work that awaited her return.

'It sounds fascinating,' Sandy said. 'Better than being stuck out in the wilds with only the monkeys and the mail-order catalogues for company!' She pulled a rueful face at Mike.

'I'd swop places any time, Sandy,' she said with feeling. 'I know I'm lucky to have such a job, but I can't tell you how tired I get of pushing through the crowds at Oxford Circus. And London's so noisy and grimy, and our garden's about the size of this table—I love the quiet here, the daily pace of life.

It seems to have a natural rhythm that most of us living in cities have quite forgotten.'

'You sound just like Brent. He's turned in his television career to farm up in the hills near the Tanzanian border. He says he's sick to death of hotels and airports and government offices. His book is a kind of valedictory, a farewell to all that. He's had this farm for years but never had the time to devote to it until now.'

She flushed. 'I didn't realise he was a guest. I'm afraid I treated him rather——' Her voice trailed away.

Mike flashed her a quick look and grinned. 'He probably deserved it. And Brent's never slow to see the humour in a situation. I wouldn't worry about it.' He looked round. 'I'm surprised he's not here tonight. We usually eat together.'

'Have you known him a long time?' The question was out before she realised it. She was surprised at herself. She thought the last thing she wanted to talk about was Brent Nicholson, yet here she was pursuing the subject.

'Years and years. We first met when I was a student hitching around Africa, and Brent gave me a lift out of Windhoek. It was meant to be to the next town, but we ended up doing a thousand miles through Namibia together. Then we bumped into each other later when I was managing a hotel out in the wilds of Tanzania. After that we kept in touch, and when I moved up here Brent became a pretty regular visitor. He's the godfather of our two boys——'

'He'd make a marvellous father,' Sandy put in, 'but if I say that, he always misquotes the Bible at me and says it's better to burn than to marry! He's a real loner, I don't think anyone will ever tie him down.' She sighed, a bit wistfully. 'I can't blame him, really. He seems to have a marvellous life, doing exactly what he wants, when he wants to.'

Mike squeezed her shoulder. 'While you, poor old thing, are stuck in this God-forsaken hole, with only your poor old broken-down husband and a staff of about a hundred to minister to your everyday needs——'

She laughed readily and looked at Kate. 'Don't get me wrong. I love my life here and I know how lucky I am. It's just that I've always envied men their freedom. It seems to me if they don't like something they can simply turn their back and walk away, while we're the ones left holding the baby!'

Kate met Sandy's eyes. She liked this couple enormously, their warmth and humour, and their gift for ready friendship. She paused. 'In my case that was literally true,' she found herself confessing. 'I was due to marry Charlie's father in the spring, but when I told him a week or two before that I was pregnant I didn't see him for dust. The last I heard he was making his fortune in Saudi Arabia!'

'And not being very forthcoming with the maintenance payments, either, I'll bet,' said Sandy.

'I didn't ask. After all, I'd allowed myself to get into the situation, so I figured I'd better stand on my own two feet from the beginning. Not that it wasn't hard at first. I can remember times when there was nothing to eat but a loaf of bread till pay day. And for years Charlie had nothing to wear but cast-offs and hand-me-downs.'

'Ours still do—although in this climate they don't need much except shorts and sandals.' Sandy grinned cherrfully at her. Then she raised a hand, looking past Kate's shoulder. 'Oh, here's Brent. Hi, come on over, we were just talking about you.'

Kate turned, saw Brent walking from the shadows on to the lamp-lit terrace, and without warning colour flushed to her cheeks and her heart hammered like a teenager's. So sudden and violent was her reaction that she had to press her hand hard to her side as if she had stitch.

'Are you all right?' Charlie had seen, and worry crossed his child's face. She nodded, unable to look away from Brent's tall figure.

He had changed into dark trousers and a white shirt and his hair still curled damply from the shower, but it was his eyes that held her as he loped towards them.

'My,' he said laconically, 'that must have been interesting.'

She managed to hold his gaze, but it was a struggle. She longed to look away, to hide the shyness and confusion that was flooding at full ebb through her.

'Mike and Sandy were just telling me you are not what you seem.' Surprisingly her voice did not shake when she spoke, but sounded coldly sardonic.

'Are any of us?' His tone was light, but she knew he had neither forgotten nor forgiven a word that had passed between them that morning.

'Here, I'll get you a chair. We've got some great steak on the menu tonight. Nairobi's best. Brought back by yours truly this morning.' Slowly his eyes went from hers to Mike. It was like having a laser beam turned off. Silently she exhaled the breath she had been holding.

'You got the boys OK?'

'No problem.'

'Good. Don't let the horrors wake me before seven. I plan to work most of tonight.' He nodded round at them, chucked Charlie under the chin, and said, 'I think I'll eat later, if you'll excuse me. I need a drink or three first.'

'What's eating him?' Mike mused. Kate watched him go, a lithe and easy figure, threading his way through the tables. She knew with certainty, although she could not have said why, that she and she alone was the reason he would not stay.

She reached for her glass and drank from it. She was less sure exactly why she felt so disappointed and disturbed. But her reaction to his appearance had thrown her completely off balance. It was as if the undercurrent of attraction she had sensed between them from the first had swollen suddenly and of its own accord into a raging flood. Her heart was still beating its deranged tattoo and only now was the heat subsiding from her cheeks. She bent her head to her plate, anxious to mask her feelings, although she sensed a speculative glance or two from Sandy.

Yet it was all completely predictable, she lectured

herself silently and logically. She was a normal woman with normal desires, however tightly they were reined in. Why shouldn't an attractive, charismatic man stir a response in her, especially when she was on holiday, relaxed, and with some of her habitual defences down?

And the fact that he set her pulses fluttering meant nothing at all. Men had no place in her life, and that was not going to change. No one need ever know how she felt, and once she was back in England it would all be a laughable holiday incident, put firmly behind her.

'What's the matter? Is there a slug in the salad?' Mike laughed. 'You're scrutinising it like Sherlock Holmes!'

She raised her head. 'Not a creepy-crawly in sight,' she retorted with a smile that hid her feelings. 'I don't know how you manage to produce food like this so far from civilisation.' As she spoke her eyes went to the place where she had last seen Brent and she saw that the night had swallowed him up; where he had been there was only empty darkness.

Much later, after Charlie had gone to bed, and a drink with Mike and Sandy at the bar led to another and then another, she made her way back towards her room. The path wound through sweet-smelling bushes and was marked by lights set into the ground which lit her feet but barely penetrated the velvet darkness.

Her head buzzed from the wine and the conversation. She felt happy and relaxingly tired, all the loneliness and confusion she had felt earlier in the evening driven back by the warm mantle of unexpected friendship that had enveloped her.

'Heh!'

'Oh!'

She gasped in shock. Part of the darkness was solid and she had walked right into it.

'Lucky I'm not an elephant,' Brent said drily. She could feel his hands on her upper arms as he steadied her.

Now, as her eyes focused, she could see his white shirt gleaming, although his face was shadowed.

'I'm all right. You don't have to hold me.'

His hands dropped slowly.

'Too drunk to see where you're going?'

'I'm perfectly sober. Don't be so insulting.'

'I'm afraid it's becoming a habit—at least where you're concerned. I would go as far as to say you bring out the worst in me.'

The glint of his eyes mocked her.

'I thought you were going to work all night.'

'I intend to. But I'm having problems with my concentration. What do you suggest I do about that?'

There was a teasing, provocative tone to his voice which set her heart thudding.

'How about a long walk, or a cold shower.'

'I'm taking the walk—it's not helping.' He stepped closer to her. 'In fact I'd say it's rather compounding the problem.'

She stepped back. 'I don't know what you're talking about.'

'Oh?' The low, husky exclamation was like a

caress of her spine. 'I somehow have a feeling you do.'

'Don't tell me what I know or don't know!'

She tried to step past him, frightened of losing her control of the situation.

He said, 'Our—disagreements—this morning left a rather sour taste in my mouth. I feel I perhaps owe you an apology.'

'Perhaps? I would say certainly.'

'All right then. I apologise. I said things I had no business to say. I was unforgivably rude. There.'

She gasped at his effrontery. There was no hint of remorse in his tone, and the way he looked at her told her his words were an empty mockery of contrition.

'I don't believe you mean a word of it!'

He shrugged carelessly. 'That's for you to decide. But at least I've had the decency to go through the motions. Now how about you?'

'What on earth do you mean?'

'I mean harsh words were said on both sides. It takes two to argue and it takes two to make up.'

'Argue! Make up!' she burst out. 'You're talking as if there's something between us! Well, there isn't. We've only just met. We're little more than strangers to each other.'

He moved closer to her, blocking her path, and his voice held the same velvet warmth as the darkness which enfolded them.

'Is that what you feel—what you really feel, Kate? Because I'm not sure that's how it is. Oh yes, it's true we've only just met, but I don't think we are strangers, I don't think we ever were. Not from that moment when you stepped out on to your balcony looking so utterly seductive in your sheet——' His mouth crooked at the memory. 'I looked at you and thought I was dreaming, to see such a vision of womanhood, at dawn, out here in the middle of nowhere. But when you turned to look at me with those huge, defensive grey eyes of yours I knew that if we hadn't met before, then we certainly should have done.'

His words made her quiver dangerously inside, and he was so close to her that she could almost feel the heat of his skin.

'Save your romantic patter for someone who might respond to it,' she said tightly. 'I've heard it all before—too often for my liking—and I'm not interested. I told you this morning, I'm not interested. I just want to be left alone.'

There was a pause. Then Brent said softly, 'Uptight and a liar to boot, Kate?'

'What!' She could scarcely believe her ears. Without thought her hand went back to strike up at the side of his cheek, but Brent caught her wrist in mid swing.

'A liar is someone who doesn't tell the truth,' he said, with exaggerated patience. 'You are not telling the truth, Kate. You might want to be left alone, but you are certainly *not* not interested. I saw what happened between us when I walked on to the terrace this evening. Your eyes gave you away. Why do you think I didn't stay? I didn't want to spoil your meal, or make you uncomfortable in front of Charlie and the others. You were obviously enjoying yourself with

Mike and Sandy. I was actually damned hungry. I still am, if you want to know. A sandwich on a tray is not very sustaining after a long, hot day in the bush.'

'I don't know what you're talking about. I might have been surprised to see you, just when the conversation happened to be about you, but surprise is rather different from the naked passion you seem to believe your presence engendered. Perhaps I ought to remind you what you said to me last night—about the arrogance of believing that every word and gesture means someone wants to get you into bed——'

'Surprised.' He repeated the word slowly, as if he had never heard it before. 'Well, maybe. If you insist.' His hand dropped from her arm and as it did so his fingertips lightly trailed the soft underside of her wrist. She trembled at the effect of the fleeting caress, and his eyes told her he had registered her response. But to her relief he stepped back.

'Perhaps you ought to get back to your work,' she said tightly.

And you to your cold cot.'

Her eyes flicked up.

'Shakespeare,' he said mockingly. 'I'm very well read for a bush-bashing game-ranger.'

She moistened her lips. 'You're right. I do owe you an apology—for mistaking your profession. I should have realised that no employee of the lodge would dare to be so damned impertinent to a guest, although I suppose it amused you to allow me to be misled like that. Or maybe you thought your face was so famous that you would be instantly recognised.'

For the first time she saw him truly angry.

'I've no interest in fame and I certainly don't expect anyone to recognise me,' he said harshly. 'My job has been to report the news, not to be a television entertainer for people too lazy to stir out of their own homes to find their amusement. But I'll tell you this, Kate Taylor, if I were a safari guide and had you to deal with, I'd bitterly resent your frosty patronage. You seem to believe that you're too good for this world, and that normal relationships with everyday mortals are quite beneath you. I have a strong hunch that that's not the real you, but if you carry on behaving as if it is, then it probably will become so, and in the end you will become a very bitter and lonely old woman. Goodnight.'

He turned and the darkness swallowed him up instantly, leaving behind only the insistent shirring of the cicadas. They echoed a buzz in her head which was outrage and anger churning her thoughts to screaming incoherence.

Bitter. Lonely. The words echoed in her brain as she stormed back towards her room. How dared he? What did he know about anything? If she were to be bitter about anything it would be the relationships she had made, not those she hadn't. And being alone didn't mean you had to be lonely. If she chose to live like that it was her business, and nothing whatever to do with interfering meddlers like Brent Nicholson!

Yet no matter how hard she fought off his words, they tolled a dismal litany in her head. That night as she lay in bed, while the hyenas and jackals began their nightly chorus, she went over and over every last detail of his cruel accusations.

She knew he was not right in his harsh judgement of her—but he was not entirely wrong, either. And it was that uncomfortable knowledge which kept her awake until dawn was approaching.

CHAPTER FOUR

IT WAS unbelievably hot. The air was thick and still, and the scents from the flowering tropical shrubs lay over the grassed lawns around the swimming-pool like a perfumed fog.

Kate lay back and felt the heat beating down on her skin and turning the curtain of her closed eyes to red.

Damn that man, she thought to herself, for the umpteenth time that day. She had vowed that she would not let him spoil her holiday, and yet his words rolled ceaselessly around her head, ruining any chance of real relaxation.

After her troubled night she had slipped into an uneasy sleep at dawn and had then overslept so that she and Charlie had missed the morning's game ride. She consoled herself with the thought that a quiet day in the lodge's luxurious grounds would do neither of them any harm, and in one way it had done a lot of good.

Arriving at the swimming-pool, Charlie had found Mike and Sandy's two boys already splashing about, and in very few minutes had managed to join in their game. They were delighted to have a new friend—Adam told Kate that most of the guests were 'absolutely ancient'. 'Like me,' she teased him, and then felt sorry when she saw a red flush of embarrassment flood his face.

Charlie was thrilled to find people his age, and when she saw how he whooped and jumped in the blue water she realised what a strain it would have been for him to have had to behave as an adult for the entire holiday.

It also gave her some unaccustomed peace to read her books and think her thoughts. Once she saw the boys were quite at home together, she settled back on a lounger. It should have been perfect, this glorious pool all to herself except for the three boys. She wore a new black bikini which flattered her tall figure and her hair was pinned high on her head to keep her face and neck cool. By her left hand was an iced lemonade, fetched for her by Charlie, and by her right was a pile of holiday reading, postcards, a pen and a handy pair of binoculars for watching the exotic bird-life.

It was the sort of scene she had sat behind her desk in noisy Oxford Street and dreamed of, but now that it was here and for real, it was not living up to expectations.

She shifted uncomfortably, her body made restless and irritable by her thoughts.

Damn the man, she thought savagely again, and opened her eyes only to see the figure that haunted her mind, in person, on the far side of the pool. As she watched she saw him pause, spring and then dive into the blue water, his body describing a perfect arc through the air. He came up in the middle of the pool and effortlessly swam the length of it several times with a powerful crawl. When he stopped, he joined the boys and was soon organising an underwater swimming competition.

His presence made her want to pick up her towel and flee. She stifled the longing, but could not discipline her eyes from straying obsessively towards him. To hide her interest, she put on her dark glasses and took up a book.

Over the top of it she saw him diving and cutting through the water, a brown, glistening body, hair swept back from his face as he surfaced.

That dangerous, subversive beating of her body started as she looked at him, and from time to time he glanced in her direction, almost as if he knew what was happening in the innermost parts of her.

She forced herself to lie back and close her eyes, and after a time the sheer force of the African sun made the shouting and splashing recede and much-needed sleep began to steal over her.

'Well, good morning.'

The lazy voice, nearby, made her eyes fly open.

Brent had swum across to her and was now resting his chin on his arms which were folded along the edge of the pool. Water ran in streams from his tanned shoulders.

'Take those glasses off and come in.'

She saw white teeth, eyes crinkled into a smile, hair slicked back from a strong face. Last night might not have happened, for all the evidence he showed of their dispute.

'I was asleep—until you woke me,' she said rudely.

'The day's too short for sleeping. It's beautiful in here, especially now those lads have gone off and left us in peace.'

She looked round. It was true. The pool, enclosed in its hedge of beautiful shrubs, was deserted except for the two of them. She saw him eyeing her, quite frankly assessing her half-naked body, and thought again about his predictions last night. Lonely? Bitter? Perversity entered, like iron, into her soul. Was that what he thought? Well, she'd show him.

Slowly she took off her glasses, meeting his eyes, and laid them beside her. Then she swung her long legs down and stood up, sensuously stretching like a cat in the sunshine, showing a figure which was unflawed. Slowly she walked to the edge of the pool, balanced for a moment, then dived smoothly into the water.

She swam easily for several lengths, feeling the power and suppleness of her muscles. She had always been a good swimmer, and she and Charlie regularly visited their local pool in London. When she stopped, Brent ducked over to join her.

'An admirable performance.'

'I wasn't performing—just swimming.'

She stood up in the waist-high water. The wetness of her bikini stretched it tight across her full breasts, but she did not turn to hide the detail of her body from Brent's obvious interest. Instead she kept her shoulders back and head high and pushed strands of wet hair back from her forehead. He stood opposite her. She saw that his chest was shadowed with dark hair which dipped to a flat stomach and lean hips. The muscles of his shoulders and arms were tanned and hard.

'An admirable swim, then.'

He seemed unable to keep his eyes from her, and as

he did so his left hand moved to check the watch on his right. It was a habitual gesture she had noticed before, but only now did it fall into place. In a world of deadlines and tight schedules, time must have been all to him.

'Damn——'

'What is it?'

'My watch. I had it a few minutes ago.' He cast around in the pool. 'It must have come off.'

She joined the hunt, and for five minutes there was silence as they both searched and dived. Then she saw it, silver and black, glinting under the deepest water. She took a breath, dived down and scooped it up, before swimming strongly back towards the shallower water.

'Here it is.' She waved it aloft, suddenly as delighted as a schoolgirl to have found the missing treasure.

Brent waded over. 'Well done. Clever girl.' She pulled the watch back away from him.

'Girl?' she said slowly. 'I hardly think so. That's as absurd as me calling you a boy.'

She felt power and confidence return to her, as tangible as the hard metal she held up in her hand. Despite the attraction she felt for Brent, she was sure she could master it. Her years of self-discipline would stand her in good stead. And meanwhile she would enjoy deflating his ego a little. He was altogether too sure of himself and the attraction of his magnetic personality.

Brent moved closer still. His hand reached for the watch and as he did so their fingers brushed. The shock was powerful, out of all proportion to the contact. She could not help but tense, and he saw it.

His eyes locked with hers. They were so close she could see the way the water ran in rivules between the hairs on his chest. His eyes were brown, then tawny, mocking her discomfort, warm with invitation.

Slowly, deliberately, he searched her face, the firm brow, grey eyes, and wide mouth, then his scan went lower, to the proudness of her neck, the flawless shoulders, the plunge of her breasts and her slim waist.

'You're no girl.' When he spoke his voice was husky.

'That's what I said.'

His fingers grasped the watch and her hand with it. He moved forward. She trembled. She was sure he was going to kiss her and she did not know what she would do if he did. Her new-found confidence wavered and seemed poised to flee in the face of the urgent cravings of her body. He brought their two hands down, stepping closer still, pulling her towards him.

'You're no girl, and I'm no boy,' he repeated, 'and we're both old enough to know what's going on between us now—it's the oldest game in the book.'

Slowly, insistently his hands took her waist beneath the sparkling water. He braced himself to pull her body to his. She longed to respond to his insistent pressure.

Go on, said a traitorous voice in her head, what harm could there be? It's only a game; he said so. And you're on holiday—enjoy yourself!

But she had played the game before, or versions of it, and every time she had lost.

She met his eyes and held them for a long moment. Then slowly, cruelly, she stepped back in the water, breaking the hold of his fingers. She held out the watch to him like Eve offering the apple.

'I know the game,' she said coolly, and she let her eyes scour his face as closely as he had earlier scanned hers. 'The only problem is—I'm not playing.'

He took the watch and snapped the bracelet over his wrist, surveying her as he did so. His mouth had set into an angry line and his eyes were dark. For a moment he did not speak, then when he did his voice was cold with contempt.

'Oh, yes you are. You're playing that other game. The one women have used against men for centuries. There are various names for it—none very polite. I'll spare your blushes by not repeating any of them, although I'm sure you've heard them before. Personally I prefer my game—it's one for adults. Yours I've always found rather adolescent.'

She flushed fiercely. She had never met a man whose words had found their mark with such unerring accuracy. No doubt his profession had given him plenty of chances to practise the barbed comment and pointed phrase.

She opened her mouth to find some savage response, although what she had no idea, when the pool suddenly erupted around them. Charlie and his new friends were diving and jumping in, shouting and laughing. So intent had they both been on their private drama that they had not seen the boys running across the grass. Charlie pulled her down under the water, and when she surfaced, spluttering, Brent had gone.

He had swum rapidly away and was already levering himself agilely up and out of the water.

'Oh, Charlie!' she cried, far more angry than the playful gesture warranted, and his face showed surprise at her unexpected bad temper.

'Only a joke, Mum,' he said, before beating a strategic retreat, looking back over his shoulder in genuine puzzlement.

Her bad mood persisted all day, and although she tried to mask it, she knew Charlie was disturbed by the way she sat silent over lunch and buried her head in a book all afternoon.

Only in the evening, when they set off in a Land Rover driven by Mike for an evening's game-viewing, and there was no chance at all of bumping into Brent, did her spirits begin to lift.

Charlie, Adam and Joe sat in the back and she joined Mike in the front and they drove companionably on a long circuit of the plains watching the abundant game.

Mike said, 'We're starting a new venture soon. Walking-safaris. You walk from one overnight camp to another, carefully protected by our guards, of course, and do a three-day tour of one of the remoter areas. They pioneered them in Zambia and it's what people seem to want now. You don't get much of a feel for the country from inside a Land Rover, and now that safari holidays are so popular it can get a bit like spaghetti junction in the high season.'

'It sounds fabulous. I remember walking through the bush with my father. He seemed to know everything about everything. There wasn't a plant he couldn't name, or a spoor he didn't recognise. That was in Zambia, along the Luangwa River.'

'I've never been there. I've always wanted to go——Look!' Mike stopped to let them watch a small tribe of mongooses play around the tunnelled ant-hill which was their home.

Kate looked down and saw, just by the Land Rover, a black dung beetle laboriously pushing a ball of dung over the grass. Its labours with the load as big as it was reminded her vividly of her own struggle to raise Charlie single-handed. Every day she had woken to the knowledge that she, and she alone, had to shoulder the burden of feeding and clothing and keeping them both, balancing the desperate need to earn a living against the constant demands of motherhood. For years she had made do with temporary jobs, bored by the few demands they made on her capabilities but needing to be free to look after Charlie when he was sick or on holiday from school.

The beetle came to a particularly challenging clump of grass. No matter how hard it pushed, it made no progress with its burden.

Sometimes it had been like that for her. There had been times when she simply could not meet their bills, or they had nowhere decent to live, patches when Charlie had seemed unhappy and she had been ravaged by guilt at his lack of a father. But just as the beetle was now over that hurdle and rolling its dung ball speedily on its way, so life had grown easier for her.

When the store she now worked for had spotted her potential and offered her a management training, life had taken a distinct turn for the better. And her recent promotion meant that she and Charlie could probably afford to have a holiday like this every year.

It was a thought that should have made her feel delighted, yet she felt oddly cast down at the prospect of year after similar year marching endlessly ahead.

'So how about it?' She jerked back to the present, realising Mike was talking to her.

'Oh Mum, can we?' Charlie was saying.

She flushed. 'I'm sorry, Mike, I didn't hear what you were saying. I was watching a dung beetle mountaineer over a clump of grass. I didn't mean to be rude.'

Mike wasn't at all put out. 'It's the little things that are often most fascinating. Most of our guests only want to see big game, but I always tell them they'll miss a lot if they only look out for lion and elephant. I just wondered if you and Charlie would like to come on a little expedition with me and the boys. I've got to do some reconnoitring for these walking safaris, and since the boys are home they might as well come with me. I know they'd love Charlie to come along, and from what you've been saying I guess you'd enjoy it as well.'

'It sounds fabulous. But I'm not sure——'

'Well, think about it. We'll probably go for about three days, that's two nights' camping, and we'll have to cover a fair bit of ground, but I can promise you some spectacular country—places that most visitors never see. You'll be quite safe, although you'd probably need to check whether your holiday insurance extends to camping expeditions. I wouldn't suggest it to most people, but with your experience of the bush——'

'Mum!' Charlie was hanging over the seat, pulling at her shoulder, willing her to say yes. 'Oh Mum, it'd be great.'

She turned and his eager face, alight with joy, melted her instinctive doubts.

'We'd love to, if it would be no trouble.'

Mike grinned. 'A pleasure.'

'What about Sandy, will she be coming?'

Mike shook his head. 'She'd love to, but one of us always has to stay on base to sort out any problems.' He turned to her, grinning cheerfully. 'But don't worry, we'll be chaperoned. I've already commandeered Brent as second driver.'

CHAPTER FIVE

'WHAT a day, eh? I'm shattered.' Mike poked the embers with a stick and put on some more wood. Brent stood up and fetched a bottle of whisky from the Land Rover.

'No glasses. We'll have to make do with mugs,' he said, pouring generous dashes into three enamel camping mugs.

Kate accepted hers without demur. The day had been hot, but now it was late and there was a bite of cold in the night air that cut through her thick sweater. The darkness closed all round their small camp, although above them the stars glittered and wheeled with a magical intensity.

She got up and checked the three boys sleeping in the tent a small distance off. They lay in their sleeping-bags packed side by side like sardines in a tin, and she smiled as she covered the torch light with her hand and shone the muted glow on to their innocent, oblivious faces.

Mike had brought the tent for her and Charlie, but when she felt how rapidly the air cooled at dusk, up here on the ridge, she insisted the three boys should have the shelter.

'I've spent dozens of nights in the open,' she assured him. 'I love sleeping under the stars.'

'We can huddle together for warmth,' Brent had said drily, and she had flashed him a hostile look, but that brief exchange had been the only visible manifestation of tension between them the whole long day.

Although when she had first heard that he would be on the trip she almost withdrew from going. Mike, seeing her look of dismay, had sought to reassure her. 'I suppose he's been pursuing you, eh?'

She shrugged, embarrassed.

'Well, Brent's never been one to resist a pretty face, and you are a bit of a stunner, Kate, but you mustn't let him worry you. Nothing's ever very serious with Brent, and I would guess you've had plenty of practice in seeing off unwelcome male advances.'

He had laughed heartily, but in her newly vulnerable state she pored obsessionally over his words.

What had he meant? Was it so clear to everyone that she had turned her heart to stone and frozen away all possible suitors over the last half-dozen years?

Did he, too, see her the way Brent saw her, tense and bitter? And what of his comments about Brent? Well, there was no news in those. She had known from the first that he was the kind of man who saw women merely as a source of transitory pleasure. So why did Mike's words make her feel so very sour and angry?

Yet she had resolved, for Charlie's sake, to put all these adult problems away for the duration of the expedition, and had forced herself to behave with friendly cheerfulness to everyone from the first.

And after the first tense hour or so, when she had

been acutely aware of Brent's speculative gaze upon her, it had been surprisingly easy.

Brent and Mike took it in turns to drive and they made good progress, soon leaving behind the last vestiges of track and striking off across open country, which grew harsher and drier as they drove further north.

Once Brent stopped and pointed. 'Reticulated giraffe,' he said, with a grin. 'There's one of your ambitions fulfilled, Kate.' The animals, with their markings as clear and distinct as a well laid crazy pavement, moved in stately single file across their vision. Charlie logged them on his list, which had now grown to three pages.

'That's where we're heading.'

Mike pointed to a thin distant smudge of greeny grey, where denser vegetation marked the line of a river. From the valley a ridge rose like the shoulder of a sleeping giant along the horizon.

'We'll sleep up there tonight. There's a few too many elephant and buffalo browsing down in the valley for my taste.'

Brent laughed. 'You mean you prefer the lion, up on the ridge?'

Kate saw Charlie's eyes seek hers for reassurance and she said, 'He's only teasing. We'll be quite safe, as long as we're sensible. Look at me. I've survived any number of safaris and my father didn't even carry a gun.'

'We've got two,' said Charlie, awed. 'And Mum, do you know, Adam and Joe can both use them.'

'They can,' Mike put in quickly, 'but they're only

allowed to when I'm supervising them.'

'I'd like to learn, though.'

She laughed. 'It wouldn't be very useful where we live. The only wildlife around there is the sparrows in the local park.' She saw his eyes darken and dull and a pang went through her. She felt exactly the same way when she thought of their cramped London flat and the grey, gritty air of the city.

They stopped at lunch time in the river valley, where kingfishers skimmed the water and glossy-leaved fig trees cast welcome shade. Kate laid out the ham and bread and fruit that Sandy had packed for them, and handed soft drinks to the boys. The two men drank thirstily from cans of beer, driving the dust of the road from their throats, before attacking the food with equal gusto.

Kate marvelled anew at just how good simple food could taste when eaten in the open, under a cloudless sky. The boys ate standing up, examining the white trunk of a fig tree which had split a granite boulder in two as it thrust its way up out of the soil.

After lunch Mike tipped his hat over his eyes and slept. Brent put up the bonnet of the Land Rover and tinkered with the engine, and Kate took Charlie's binoculars and wandered off to the sandy cliff at the edge of the sleepy river.

She wanted to check that the black bumps she had spotted in a pool further downstream were what she thought they were, and she was delighted to focus the glasses and see the noses and twitching ears of a school of lazing hippo. When she listened carefully she could also hear their snuffling grunts above the soaring chorus of bird-song all around.

'It's a good job we didn't light a fire.'

Brent had come up behind her.

'Why?'

She was too surprised at his comment to feel edgy at his presence.

'For some reason hippo hate fire. There's any number of accounts of how they come out of the water and try to stamp it out—and anything else that gets in the way at the time. They aren't nearly as cuddly and harmless as they look.'

'They can be quite tame, though, can't they? I once heard of a hotel keeper in Zambia who used to give one a beer every night. At eight o'clock on the dot the animal would waddle up out of the river and open its great jaws and the man would pour in a can of beer, and then the hippo would twitch its tail and waddle off again.'

Brent laughed. 'I've heard that story, too. In my version the animal drank it bottle and all. I think it's one of the great bush tales of Africa. By the time these stories have been told and re-told nobody knows how much is fact and how much is fiction.'

'Well, I'm going to carry on believing it. It's a nice story.'

She raised the binoculars again, scanning the scene, sighing as she did so. 'I love this kind of country. I can't imagine why you gave up being a game-ranger. Mike said that's what you used to do.'

She turned, a little apprehensive. It seemed strange to be talking like this, without the antagonism that had marred all their previous encounters, and yet the long, companionable morning had somehow made it possible. Brent was leaning against a tree, his hands thrust into his jeans pockets, his hat shading his face.

'Mike's right. I was a ranger, but years ago. The people I worked for sent me off to university to study conservation science but I pretty quickly switched to politics and economics. I suppose the truth is that the activities of people came to interest me more than the doings of animals.

'After that I just drifted into journalism, writing for newspapers, and then got head-hunted for television.'

He grinned, she could see the gleam of his teeth in the shadow of his hat brim. She was glad she could not see his eyes, it made it easier to talk.

'I suppose the face fitted,' he said loconically, 'and I knew my way around Africa—where to bribe my way in, where to bribe my way out—that sort of thing.'

'You make it sound awful.'

'Bribery's not awful, just a fact of life. There are plenty of worse things——'

'What do you mean?'

'I hardly know where to start.'

She turned back to him again. This time she could see his eyes, and they were dark and serious, all flirtation driven from them.

'You could try,' she said tentatively.

'Are you really interested?'

'Yes!' There was an intensity in her tone that surprised even herself. 'Yes,' she said more quietly. 'I really am.'

'Well, let's see, there are all the small, forgotten

wars that devastate thousands of people's lives every year but which no one gives a damn about because they've never even heard of the places involved. And there are the droughts, and the over-grazing, and the way the desert is spreading out over decent land all the time. There's the illness and the poverty and the racism—whites hating blacks, and blacks hating whites, and that's before you get on to all the various shades of yellow and brown. Then there's the corruption—oh, not the single banknote folded inside a passport, that's just a minor irritation, but the big-scale stuff, the ministers and the businessmen salting away millions in their Swiss bank accounts while half the people in their countries are starving.'

'Is it really like that?' Her eyes were wide.

'Yes,' he said. Then he added, 'And no. There's the other side of the coin as well. I've had more warmth and generosity shown to me by people living on the breadline out here than by people living comfortably in London or New York. And there's any number of people working themselves to a shadow trying to improve living conditions, or risking their lives by standing up against regimes they disapprove of.

'I suppose the truth is that people are people wherever they live. It's just that Africa seems to sharpen the contrasts.' He sighed. 'I'm feeling jaded at the moment, so I suppose I tend to see the bad rather than the good. I'm not an objective witness.'

She turned away, scanning the river which seemed to tremble in the midday heat. 'Is that why you're giving up television reporting? Mike said your book was a swan-song.'

'Partly. What I see on assignments now makes me dispirited and depressed, so I tend not to do a very good job. But I'm also bored.' He levered himself away from his tree and moved to stand beside her, and his voice lightened to its more habitual teasing tone. 'I'm a restless spirit, Kate. Nothing seems to satisfy me for that long.'

'What comes next?'

'My farm. You should just see it, it's beautiful. Up in the hills with views like you can't imagine from the veranda. I've had it for years, but I've had to leave it in the hands of a manager until now.'

'And what happens when you get bored with that?' she said, with an edge to her voice. She would love to see his farm, but she never would. And his careless, roving attitude to life clashed uncomfortably with the harsh daily grind which was all she had known.

'I don't know—I don't know if I shall. I feel as if I've done enough travelling to last a lifetime, and farming is different from journalism, you can't just pick it up and drop it as the whim takes you. If you plant a tree it takes decades to grow——' His voice tailed off as if his mind was already busy planning and reorganising. Then he laughed. 'I guess it's old age catching up with me at last. I seem to have an unaccountable new urge to put down roots.'

'Or maybe just maturity,' she put in, with asperity.

He gave her a sidelong look. 'Ow,' he said softly.

She caught her breath. She had vowed to put aside the tension that lay between them, but now it rose up again, threatening immediately their new-found equilibrium.

'I'm sorry,' she said quickly. 'I had no right to say that.'

'It's all right. It's true,' he said. Then, without looking at her, he said, 'But what about you? I've been doing all the talking. I don't even know what you do.'

She explained about the store, aware that her voice sounded dull and flat. When she finished he said, 'You don't sound very thrilled by it all.'

'I don't want to bite the hand that feeds me,' she said. 'I'm very grateful to have been given the chance, and the training—after all I only started there as a temporary shop assistant.'

'Grateful be damned,' he said. 'They didn't promote you out of the goodness of their hearts. They'll have got far more out of their investment in you than you'll ever see.'

His bluntness startled her. She thought of the nights she worked late at home, reading papers and drafting proposals, the Saturday meetings she attended without protest, and the nights she lay awake worrying over the fine detail of current projects. Perhaps he was right. She had been so bowled over by the change in her fortunes, so thrilled by the security and the steady rise in her salary, that she had never considered the other side of the equation.

'I suppose so.'

'So what's wrong with it all?'

'I don't know,' she began hesitantly, fumbling for words. She had never explained her feelings to anyone before, not even herself. 'I think it's a bit like working in a chocolate factory. At first you can't get enough of the stuff, but later you grow sick of the sight of it. The store's full of wonderful things—clothes and furniture and jewellery. When you first go there you long to buy everything, then you get used to it and you realise you don't want any of it. Then later on you grow to hate the sight of it all.

'Sometimes I look at the customers frantically buying things and I wonder just how much they really want or need what they're getting, and yet my job is to make people want more, spend more, buy more. Sometimes I walk through the departments and I feel as if I'm choking because the air's so thick and perfumed, and outside it's just the same. People everywhere, and traffic, and noise, and not a blade of grass in sight!'

'"Getting and spending, we lay waste our powers",' Brent said softly. 'Wordsworth. I can't remember how it goes on.'

'I've got a wardrobe full of designer clothes at home. I have to have them for my job, but I'm a million times happier on this trip, with just a change of shirt and a kettleful of water to wash in!'

Brent laughed. 'I still bet you're first in the shower when we get back to the lodge.'

She blushed, embarrassed by her outburst. 'I suppose you just think I've got romantic notions about the wilds of Africa——'

'No, I don't. Not at all. I can see by what you do, the way you walk and talk out here, the way you dress, that you know what you're doing. Charlie's learning, too. He copies you. Have you noticed how he's stopped shouting out every time he sees something exciting?'

She smiled, relieved the conversation had moved to firmer ground.

'He's a good boy.'

'He's got a good mother.'

She glanced up, surprised. His words were like an unexpected gift, making her flush with pleasure.

'Thank you.'

For the briefest moment their eyes locked but Brent instantly broke the moment, and she was glad. 'Praise where it's due,' he said lightly, lifting an eyebrow. 'Come on, we'd better get back or they'll think the crocs have got us.'

Mike was awake when they got back, and packing up.

'I just want to do a recce along here before we go,' he said. 'I thought we could do it in two groups to save time. Brent, if you take Charlie and Kate along that way, the boys and I will go the other. You know what I'm looking for, a nice level site, some shelter, but not too thick, and away from any chance of flooding. We'll go about a mile or two each way and meet back here at half-past three.'

Charlie was tense with excitement at the prospect of his first foot-safari.

'Follow Brent,' she instructed him, 'and try and walk as quietly as possible. Don't step on dry sticks unless you have to and do whatever he tells you. I'll be behind you.'

Brent led the way, his rifle on his shoulder. Soon the Land Rover was out of sight and they were alone in the wilderness, with only the sounds and sights of the animal kingdom for company.

Kate walked in a trance of delight, smelling the plants and the river, watching the birds, seeing Brent's easy gait ahead of her and knowing she felt completely safe in his hands. Every now and then he stopped to touch Charlie's arm and silently point out a monkey high in a tree, or a crocodile sleeping on a sandbank on the far side of the water.

Then, as they went to enter a glade of fig trees, he stopped them with an urgent motion of his arm. Slowly he edged forward, stopped, then went on another pace or two. After some moments he beckoned them on, indicating they should be as quiet as possible. Standing together they peered through the screen of branches on to a scene of such innocent peace and beauty that Kate felt tears prick at her eyes.

There, on emerald grass, dappled by sunlight, a young cow elephant stood with her baby, her trunk gently caressing its back and head. The little one, still covered with a fuzz of baby hair, bumped its head gently against its mother's knee in sleepy delight.

The two beasts stood almost motionless, although the cow constantly lifted her head and cast about, ever watchful.

They watched for some moments, entranced. Brent looked to Kate, over Charlie's head and they smiled at each other. Then he waved them back and they retreated with painful caution, pace by careful pace, until they could turn and make their way back towards the Land Rover.

Now, when Mike asked her how she had enjoyed the day, she could say with total honesty that she had loved every minute. 'Especially the elephant. I wish you could have seen them, Mike. It was like something out of Eden. Charlie couldn't believe we could get so close without being seen. It was wonderful for him.'

'He's out like a light now, isn't he? They all are. I'll be joining them soon.' Brent proffered the bottle to him across the flames, but he shook his head. 'I promised Sandy I'd try and get some reasonable nights. She knows what it can be like out in the bush. When you start talking and passing a bottle around a campfire it can be dawn before you know it. I've had too many mornings with eyelids like lead and a tongue like sandpaper.'

'Ah, that's what marriage does for you,' said Brent, mock-mournful. 'Thickens the waistline and dulls the stamina.'

She picked up her mug and realised Brent had refilled it without asking her.

'Rubbish. You're talking through your hat. There's nothing like it,' Mike said comfortably. 'My life wouldn't be worth living without Sandy and the boys.' He got up and collected plates to take over to the vehicle. 'And if you two start chewing the fat we'll see who's in best shape in the morning.'

He moved out of the circle of light and the darkness seemed to edge in closer around the two of them. Somewhere a hyena hooted mournfully.

'Scared?' Brent asked.

'No. I'm far more scared in London. We live in a ground-floor flat. I keep a cricket bat by my bed.'

She laughed but he didn't. 'It can't be much fun rearing a child alone in the city.'

'It's a lot of things, but fun isn't one of them.'

'What about Charlie's father?'

'What about him?' Bitterness edged her voice.

'Doesn't he play any part?'

She looked up at him, over the rim of her mug which she cradled in two hands. He sat cross-legged, one hand playing abstractedly with the bracelet of his watch, his eyes on hers.

'Am I being interviewed?'

'Of course not. I'm just curious.'

'No,' she said shortly, 'no part at all.'

She took a gulp or two from her drink and felt the spirit warm her.

Brent said nothing. From somewhere she heard her own voice offering, 'There's no great secret about it all. I'll tell you the whole story if you like.'

He nodded slowly. 'I would like.'

CHAPTER SIX

SHE said, 'I was eighteen when I had Charlie. I was engaged to Charlie's father. We had known each other for years. We'd grown up together, been to the same schools. My mother knew his mother and they were both very keen on the marriage.

'I thought I knew him inside out and backwards. He was three years older than me, and he seemed very confident and sure of himself. We'd planned to get married in April, but after all those years together the waiting got too much——' She faltered, unsure of the right words to use. 'We went to bed together, just once, but it was enough. I found out I was pregnant only weeks before the wedding, but when I broke the news, that was it. He vanished. He just packed a suitcase and ran. He was studying to be an engineer at the time, and he must have finished his training because five years later I got a letter from the Gulf where he was working on a new hospital.'

Even as she spoke she could see the pages of blue airmail paper in front of her eyes, with the small, spidery writing, and could remember the disgust with which she had thrown them on the fire. Brent said nothing, waiting.

'It was a pathetic document, full of guilt and self-pity. I guess he'd been drinking when he wrote it. He wanted me to forgive him for what he'd done. It was all about how terrible he felt, but there wasn't a word about Charlie, or me, or how things might have gone for us, except for a sweeping offer of any money we wanted.' She swallowed the bile back in her throat. 'And even that was just to show me how well he was doing in the Middle East. It made me feel ill when I read it—and disgusted with myself for ever having contemplated marrying someone so weak and self-centred.'

'And did you forgive him?'

She shook her head. 'I threw the letter on the fire. Three years ago, when my mother died, I saw him at the back of the church. But he didn't have the courage to come up and speak to me, and since then there's been no contact.'

'Everyone makes mistakes when they're eighteen,' Brent said. 'We've got nothing to go on, no experience by which to judge people. You were just unlucky——'

'Or lucky. Charlie has been the best thing in my life.'

'What about after that? Surely that can't have turned you off mankind for life?'

'No.' She turned down the corners of her mouth wryly. 'It took a little more than that. For two years when I first moved to London I had a relationship with a man——' She paused, surprised at how readily the words were tumbling out. 'I was very hard up, lonely, worried about looking after Charlie. He was ten years older than me, very steady and kind and supportive——' She looked up, challenging Brent with her eyes. 'He wasn't around all that much; I thought he was simply keen on preserving his independence, and that suited me very well. I didn't want to move in with him, or anything like that, but it was nice to have someone around and I was sure he wouldn't just vanish overnight. Then I got a phone call—from his wife.'

Bitterness came down over the years to twist her voice.

'You had no idea?'

She paused for a long time, remembering small clues and descrepancies. 'He told me a lot of lies,' she said simply, 'and I suppose I chose to believe them.'

'And then?' said Brent.

'Then nothing, for a long time. I was so hurt, my confidence so shaken, I vowed I wouldn't get involved with anyone ever again. And I didn't. I learned to stand on my own feet, make my own decisions. It worked for a time. Then when life became less of a struggle I decided it was time to do something for myself. I started to take evening classes—basic computing—and fell hook, line and sinker for my tutor.'

She took a gulp of the fiery liquid in her mug. 'Oh I knew it was corny. I had no intention of letting it get serious, but we got on so well we started to see a lot of each other. I told him about Charlie and he said he quite understood. He insisted that he loved me, and that he would love any child of mine—so I invited him home for a weekend with us. Two days later I got a letter saying the whole thing was over.'

She looked at Brent. 'He just couldn't cope with the reality of a strapping great six-year-old. He resented

Charlie's presence and the time I had to give to him—I know it's understandable, but that man promised me the moon and I was foolish enough to believe him. Yet at the first glimpse of difficulty he took to his heels. And that was it.'

She held Brent's eyes. After a time she said slowly, 'I don't want to be lied to, or hurt, or let down ever again. And I don't intend to let myself.'

Brent said, equally emphatically, 'You can't condemn half the human race from three examples.'

'Why not?' she replied crisply.

'It's not a wide enough sample.'

'It's a hundred per cent of my experience.'

'Perhaps there was a basic flaw in the choices.'

'What do you mean?'

He spread his hands, long fingers extended in exasperation. 'I don't know, exactly. I accept you've had a rotten time, but the choices were yours. I have a psychologist friend who would say you were deliberately punishing yourself for your error of judgement the first time around. He would say you wanted to prove to yourself that the male of the species was all bad, and so you deliberately set out to find examples that proved the point.

'My own view of life tends to be more simple. It sounds to me as if having Charlie closed down your options in a major way. You weren't free to go out, have fun, like other girls your age, and so you simply didn't meet the same range of people you would otherwise have done. When you did get into a relationship, you invested everything in it—and then you were let down hard. It could have been bad luck, it could have been bad judgement. Most likely it was a mixture of the two. Whatever it was, I'm sure of one thing——' He cocked an eyebrow at her in the flickering light.

'What's that?' She felt raw and shaky, pinned open on an operating table with all her bleeding wounds exposed.

'I'm sure it's not right for you to shut yourself off, as you've done. Oh, there'll be no more hurt, any more. But neither will there be any excitement, any exploration, growth—any possibility of future happiness.'

'I'm perfectly happy.' Her voice rose tight in her throat. 'At least I was, until——'

'Listen to me, Kate.' Brent's voice was low and urgent, piercing to her brain. 'You're a lovely woman. No, not just lovely. Stunning. You're strong and courageous and proud. But unless you learn to trust your own strength, unless you learn that it's something in you that no one can take away——' He broke off. 'It's none of my business, but I hate to see waste—of beauty or talents—and I know that the woman you are could all too easily start to harden.'

'No! Stop it! I've heard enough!'

She was on her feet, her mug sprawling, shouting down at him. 'How dare you keep interfering in my life? I don't need to be lectured by you! Look at how you live your life! Whenever you get bored you simply move on to something else. No doubt it's the same with people. Pick them up, use them, and discard them! Well, what sort of life is that? What the hell makes you think you've got all the answers?'

She turned blindly and began to head off into the darkness.

'Kate, for God's sake!' Brent hissed behind her, but she ran faster, tripping and stumbling over hidden logs and twisting her ankle in animal burrows. Her heart raced and anger squeezed her chest so that she could barely breathe. Air rasped in her throat as she struggled blindly on, and to her dismay she felt the wet film of furious tears on her cheeks.

How dare he? she thought. How dare he? but his words were echoing in her head with a truth and resonance that she could not deny. 'Oh!' In her panic and rage she had cannoned straight into a thorn tree. She reeled back, stumbled against a boulder on the ground, tripped and fell sprawling.

'Oh!' she cried again, winded, and then shock and anger and pain overwhelmed her in a helpless storm of crying. She laid her head on the ground and for the first time in years gave herself up to racking sobs that shook her whole body.

She had no idea how long she lay like that on the ground, but when, at last, her tears began to abate, an uncomfortable new awareness of her predicament crept in on her.

Here she was, out alone in darkness, with no idea at all of which direction the camp lay in. She levered herself up into a sitting position, her skin prickling. When she listened carefully she could hear the small rustlings of nocturnal animals. Snakes, she thought suddenly and began to feel truly frightened. Snakes slept through the heat of the day, and hunted at night, slithering through the grasses and fallen leaves until they found warm flesh to prey on. She shuddered and stood up quickly, lifting one foot, then another. Under normal circumstances she was cool-headed about such dangers, but now she felt only mounting panic.

Then she heard a larger noise, a small but distinct cracking of twigs that heralded the movement of some larger animal. She listened so intently she seemed to hear the stars humming faintly above her. It was definitely something moving, and definitely coming nearer.

'Oh.' It was a tiny sob of fear. It could be a lion, or an elephant, or, worse still, a lone bull buffalo. The noise came relentlessly nearer but she did not know which way to move for safety. Her heart hammered until she almost failed to breathe. 'Oh——' A desperate, choking noise was torn from her throat in her terror.

'Kate?' Brent's voice came out of the darkness.

'Oh!' she gasped again, relief shuddering through her.

'Kate? Oh, thank goodness!'

A piece of the darkness moved towards her, and arms went round her at once, gathering her tight to him. She felt warmth and safety and strength wrapping round her like a cloak and could not have resisted the comfort of his embrace even if she had tried.

Without thought her arms went round his waist to let him pull her closer. She felt one of his hands spread across her back, the other he held away from their bodies, and she knew he carried his rifle.

His mouth was against her hair. 'Oh, my God, I

was worried! You shouldn't have gone like that.'

For answer she buried her head harder into his shoulder.

'I shouldn't have said the things I did. If I'd known the reaction——'

She said nothing, she could not speak. The release from fear had left her weak and open, and now she could think of nothing but the feel of him holding her close, his legs braced to hold her weight, their bodies pressed together.

She had forgotten how good such closeness could feel, forgotten the force with which her body could start to beat out its own insistent needs. Or maybe she had never known. Nothing in her life before had made her feel quite like this. She longed to twist in his arms to get closer to him. She smelt woodsmoke on his jersey, felt the rough weave of wool against her cheek, and ached for him to kiss her.

When he did it was all she had longed for, and more. His head bent to hers and his lips were cool and firm, kissing her long and slowly.

Then he broke away, bent to lay his gun down carefully on the ground away from them both, and turned back. This time he could hold her fully, with both hands. He spread his hands up her back, grasping each shoulder, holding her gently and carefully before finding her lips again. As he kissed fully and more powerfully his embrace tightened about her, but there was in it a sensual respect that melted her utterly. She knew, as she received his kiss, that it was her and her alone he was kissing, and that he did not forget that, even as his lips parted hers and his tongue explored her mouth.

She kissed him back, opening to him, yielding against him. It felt so good, so right. She longed for the touch of his hands on her naked skin, ached for him, for the fulfilment his embrace promised.

But he tore his lips from hers, resting his forehead on her shoulder while his breathing steadied.

'I've wanted to do that since I first set eyes on you,' he said. 'Do you remember, on your balcony the first morning you were here. It was all I could do not to vault over the wall and take you in my arms there and then.'

Even now she said nothing. She still did not trust her voice, sure it would be as shaky as her legs. He lifted his head to search her eyes, but she turned her face away, scared of what he might read there.

And, feeling how she trembled in the chill night air, he bent for his gun and said only, 'Let's get back.'

CHAPTER SEVEN

THEY were bouncing along the bed of a dried-up watercourse, the Land Rover lurching this way and that, as Brent negotiated the boulder-strewn sand.

Kate sat in the back with Adam and Joe and tried to keep her eyes from straying to the chestnut hair and wide shoulders of the man in front of her.

Now she knew what it felt like to tangle her fingers in that hair, and to spread her hands over the muscles of that back. But she had to put it out of her mind. She had to.

Last night should never have happened. It was a mere moment of weakness, an aberration born out of the raw honesty of their confrontation across the campfire. And then she had been weak and frightened, alone in the dark, and Brent had taken advantage of her distress. Except, of course, he hadn't. All he had done was to kiss her. And when their embrace grew heated it was he who had broken it off, and led her back to camp.

If she had had her way last night, she reflected grimly, almost anything could have happened.

It had not been possible, after that, to wriggle into her sleeping-bag next to the fire, flanked by Brett and Mike in their sleeping-bags, and to fall into an easy slumber.

She had lain for a long time on her back staring up at the huge arch of stars, blocking her churning thoughts by trying to puzzle out the constellations.

Once, directly above her, a shooting star shot briefly across the firmament before fading to darkness. That was how things should be between the two of them, she thought. A brief, flaring encounter and then nothing.

She glanced across at the black, muffled shape that was Brent. He lay on his side, with his back to her, the rifle within reach of his hand, and although he was still, she knew with absolute certainty that he was not asleep but staring into the darkness thinking his thoughts. What those were she had no idea, although she longed to know.

As for Mike, he slept soundly, and if he knew anything of what had passed between them, there was no sign.

At night she had dreaded the morning, and having to face Brent again, but the routine of breaking camp made it easy to keep busy. She occupied herself cooking bacon and eggs for everyone, and although she felt Brent looking at her she was able to avoid his eyes, while the excitement and chatter of the three boys made a useful blind to her confused feelings and helped to keep the conversation light and general.

Now it was late afternoon and they were heading for a spot which Mike had earmarked as a possible permanent campsite. He was in high spirits, having that morning found an ideal place for the main base camp, and was whistling through his teeth as he scanned the bush for the place where they needed to turn off.

'Here we are.'

'That's quite a good track,' said Brent.

'It's an old hunting-trail. That poaching gang we caught last season used it as their main route through these parts.'

Brent swung the vehicle on to the rough road and stopped. 'Joe, you have a go. I'm sure you could cope with this. Is that all right, Mike?'

'Gosh!' Charlie's eyes were wide with wonder. 'Can you really drive a Land Rover?'

'I can, too,' boasted Adam.

'They've been practising since they were tall enough to reach the pedals,' said Mike. 'We're lucky here. We don't have to worry about age limits.'

'I bet you could easily learn,' Joe said soothingly to Charlie. 'Couldn't he, Dad?'

'I'm sure he could, but there's no time for lessons now. Come on, Joe, out you get.'

The boy jumped down and Brent got into the back, next to her. His shirt was dark with sweat and the familiar man-smell of him roused a sudden scalding stab of desire in her.

To keep her eyes from his she watched Charlie closely and saw the naked longing and envy with which he watched Joe start the Land Rover and cautiously put it into gear.

They had no car, she thought; in fact she couldn't even drive. Now that he was growing up there were so many things she couldn't give him—driving lessons were the least of it.

She sighed and Brent glanced across to her and for a swift, heart-stopping moment their eyes locked together, both thinking about what had passed between them the night before. Then, of accord, they looked quickly away.

Joe drove to their next stop, a small plain of rough scrub, dotted with thicker patches of thorn bush.

'There was a lot of lion around here earlier this year,' Mike warned. 'I need to reconnoitre, but it might be better if you boys stayed in the Land Rover.'

'Oh, Dad!' they pleaded in unison. 'You let us come with you last year when we were up here, do you remember?'

'All right, then.' Mike gave in without a struggle. 'But remember, you walk close behind me, single file, and you do exactly what I say—no arguing. Charlie, I suppose you want to come too?' Charlie nodded eagerly.

'Well, ask your Mum.'

She nodded her assent.

'We'll all go, then. OK, Brent?'

It was the hardest and most serious bush walking they had done. Out on the open grassland there were buck grazing everywhere, along with fat-rumped zebras and the occasional languid giraffe, but when the thorn scrub grew thicker it was hard to see far ahead.

Once Mike stopped them all with a wave of his hand, raised his binoculars, then pointed to a dense shadow under a flat-topped acacia tree. It was a single lioness, peacefully dozing, and they skirted around her, taking care to stay downwind of her so their scent would not alert her to human presence.

After a time Mike stopped and took some photos of the area where he wanted to establish another camp.

Their neat single file had scattered out as they waited for him to finish. Adam and Joe were scrambling up a turreted termite-hill twice as big as they were. Charlie had wandered a small way off and was examining with wonder the myriad small weaver-bird nests that hung from a thorn tree. Kate stood by Adam and Joe feeling the sun beat down on her head and watching the glorious flashing purple and powder-blue of the roller-birds. Nearby, Brent shifted from foot to foot, scanning about them.

'I feel uneasy and I don't know why,' he said, half to himself. Kate looked at him, as tense and alert as any wild creature. No one else seemed to have heard. She, too, looked around, her eyes trying to pierce the shadowed scrubland. Suddenly a grey area which she had taken to be a shadow moved. She saw an outline of an ear, a trunk.

'Elephant!' she whispered urgently to Brent. Even as she spoke, there was a cracking in the bushes nearby.

'Oh Lord!' Brent said. 'A herd.' He beckoned urgently to Mike and the boys, his eyes going constantly back to the one animal they could see, and began to walk backwards, his gun half lifted to cover them as they made their retreat.

Her heart racing, she followed him, urging Charlie to do the same with an urgent movement of her hand. Any moment she expected to hear a wild trumpeting and trampling as the animals got wind of them, but after a moment or two they had regained the edge of the open savannah land and Brent felt confident enough to turn to face the front again. Just as he did so they all saw the huge, lowering black shape of a rhinoceros ahead.

The animal's nostrils twitched. It put its great prehistoric head down.

'Oh, no,' said Mike, 'it's going to charge. Out of its path, everyone! Quickly! Come on, you boys, *run!*'

All she could remember was confusion. She was rooted to the spot, watching Charlie to safety, when the ground started to judder and there was a rumbling like a landslide. Brent grabbed her wrist and flung her roughly back behind the cover of a tree. From there she saw the boys sprinting nimbly towards some nearby termite-mounds, but Charlie, running, caught his foot in some rough ground and was felled on the spot, right in front of the galloping rhinoceros. She felt sick. Everything seemed to be slowed to quarter-speed. Through a roaring in her ears she heard Brent yell to Mike, 'I'll go,' and saw him dive towards the fallen boy, pulling and dragging him away just seconds before the animal trampled blindly past, thundering away from them into some bushes.

She crumpled on the spot, her knees too weak to hold her.

'He's gone,' Mike said. His face was pale. 'Are you two all right?'

Brent rolled over on to his back and lay like a dead creature. 'Phew,' he said. 'It's a good job your foot wasn't trapped, Charlie. I'd have pulled it right off.'

Charlie got up unharmed, but too shaken to speak.

Mike said to Brent, 'I could have got him if I'd had to, I had a pretty good line, but I didn't want to have to shoot with all these people about.'

Kate went and held Charlie, relieved to see colour coming back into his face. 'Are you all right?'

'Oh, Mum, it was all my fault—I feel awful.'

'Rubbish,' said Brent, from where he was lying. 'It could have happened to anyone. Look what you went down in.' He pointed to a small, lethal burrow half hidden by dry grasses.

'What about you, Brent? Are you all right?'

He looked at her, brown eyes on hers, and she saw that despite his apparant composure he, too, was pale beneath his tan. 'A bruised shin or two. Nothing worse.'

He sat up and they all gathered round, regaining their breath. Mike passed Brent his hip-flask. 'That was really unlucky,' he said. 'Elephant and rhino together.'

'At least it was the rhino that charged, and not the elephant,' Brent said and took a gulp of brandy. 'Luckily they're as blind as bats and can only travel in straight lines. Elephants can turn on a sixpence. Still,' he added cheerfully, 'I've known worse.'

'What?' said Joe. He and Adam seemed remarkably unconcerned by the whole episode, thought Kate, as she covertly monitored Charlie's face for shock.

'Well, I once jumped over a dead trunk and found a lioness and six cubs enjoying the shade on the other side.'

'What happened?' said Adam.

'Nothing.' Brent laughed. We were both too surprised to cause trouble. I just backed off as fast as I could, and she let me go.'

'Dad once had to shoot a buffalo that was about to go for him, didn't you, Dad?'

Mike said, 'I wasn't very proud of that—it was my own stupid fault for not seeing him in time. But to bump into both elephant and rhino at the same time——' he shook his head '—that's really going it. OK, son?' He cuffed Charlie gently, who nodded quietly. 'Then let's get going. I want to get you all back in one piece tomorrow.'

Later that night she went to look at Charlie sleeping peacefully in the tent, apparently none the worse for his scrape.

She stood for a long time staring down at him, and felt an icy hand squeeze her heart when she thought of the very different ending the day could have had if the rhino had been allowed to trample his fragile boy's body. He was so precious to her, beyond words!

Perhaps even more than most sons to their mothers. He was all she had in the world, the only person she dared let herself love without restraint.

Love. Her thoughts went to Brent, as they had done all day, wayward and undisciplined. What was it she felt for him? She did not know. Only that he had got right into her head, her every thought, with his irritating habit of voicing the abrasive truth, and that when she looked at him she felt weak with the need to have his arms hold her close again.

But it was a one-sided need. Although he had kissed her last night, this evening he had hardly seemed to know or care that she was there. When they stopped at nightfall to camp alongside the track back to the lodge, he had kept busy cleaning his gun and checking over the Land Rover. He had eaten his meal in near-silence, exchanging desultory words with Mike about matters of African politics and economics of which she knew nothing, and never glancing in her direction.

Perversely, his withdrawal of interest roused hers to fresh heights. Despite all her efforts, her eyes strayed constantly to his lean figure sitting easily cross-legged in the firelight. Her gaze sought his face, the planes of his cheeks, the straight, strong mouth, the wayward hair glinting in the flickering flames. She both feared and longed to catch his glance, but his eyes were shadowed and preoccupied.

He was a man of so many parts, she thought. His usual manner was cheerful, direct and teasing, and when he was like that his face was mobile and good-humoured. She remembered how readily his mouth crooked to a one-sided grin, or one eyebrow was raised in quizzical response. But he could be harsh, and in that mood his face was set and his eyes hard and penetrating.

Now, though, there was a brooding sensuality about his withdrawn and shuttered expression that made her long to trace his lips with her fingers and push her fingers gently through his hair. Her eyes went down to his hands nursing the enamel camp mug of whisky. From time to time the fingers of his hand touched his watch, the now-familiar gesture that tonight made her all too desolately aware of what little time they had together slipping away.

Now she straightened up and closed the flaps of the boys' tent. Above the wood-smoke smell of the dying fire she scented cigar smoke. A small distance away she saw a hunched figure sitting on a log, the red glow of an ember in its hand, and knew it was Brent.

'I didn't know you smoked,' she said quietly. She hadn't intended to approach him, but her feet seemed to have developed minds of their own.

'There's a great deal about me you don't know.'

He didn't turn as she stood beside him, and she knew she should go away. But she didn't.

'I just wanted to thank you for what you did this afternoon. You saved Charlie's life. I don't know what I would have done if anything had happened to him.'

There was a pause before he replied, as if he was following a line of thought, then he said, 'He would have been all right. Mike could have shot that rhino if he'd had to. Don't worry, you're in good hands. You'll both get safely back to London, and then what tales you'll have to tell your friends.' His voice twisted with sarcasm.

'Why are you being like this? Is it something I've said?'

He suddenly stood up, dashing his cigar to the ground and grinding it under his foot, and said harshly, 'No, Kate, it isn't something you've said—I'm merely doing what you have asked me repeatedly to do, leaving you alone. And I'll thank you for returning the courtesy.'

She looked up at him, the hostile eyes just an inch or two above her own and as their gazes met her heart jolted inside her.

'Perhaps I've changed my mind.' She spoke hesitatingly, not knowing she was going to say that.

'Well, change it back again. For your own sake.'

'Brent——' She put a hand on his arm. He removed it.

'Kate.' He spoke less harshly, but his voice was still cool. 'Don't you see? You're grateful to me because of what happened this afternoon. And these nights out in the bush can be a romantic time. You're forced to live cheek by jowl with strangers—things happen that wouldn't normally, not in everyday life. Believe me. I've seen it often enough over the years. But afterwards——'

'Stop it! I'm not a child. I don't need patronising like this.'

'Then face up to the truth!' His face blazed as he shouted roughly at her. 'You know what this is all about. I fancy you like crazy. I have done since the moment I set eyes on you. To put it as bluntly as I know how, I want you. I want you very, very much. I want to take you to bed and make love to you. I want to know every inch of you. But what then?'

He turned away from her and sat on the log, his elbows on his knees, his hands linked. 'Those men you talked about, last night. The ones who let you down so badly—I understand them. I'm just the same. I don't want to be tied down, to have to feel responsible for anyone but myself. The only difference between them and me, Kate, is that I'm honest enough to admit it, and I've always put my cards on the table from the start.'

'Then we both know where we are.' Her voice was little more than a whisper. His words had shaken her, but the need to have him touch her, hold her again was more urgent than any considerations of caution and good sense.

He shook his head. 'Oh, no. You say that now, but you would regret it later. I know it.'

She hugged herself. The night was cold, despite her sweater. Slowly the cold seemed to take the fever from her, to calm her head. She sighed. Sense began to return. She was silent. After a time Brent crooked his head to look at her. His eyes sought hers and he crooked his mouth in wry sadness.

'You're right,' she said, and shivered deeply.

'It's not my normal practice to turn down such enticing offers. I hope you realise it's a compliment, not an insult. You're very special, Kate, and I don't want to hurt you more than you've been hurt already.'

She nodded, bleakly.

'Here.' He stood up and peeled off his own sweater. 'Army surplus. Not very grand, but it serves its purpose.' He handed it to her.

'What about you?' she said, putting it on. Its warmth was a poor substitute for the warmth of his embrace, but it comforted her to wear it. He was wearing only his cotton bush shirt and his forearms were bare.

'I'm OK. I'm tough.' He moved along the log, making room for her to sit down, then turned to look at her in the darkness. 'You do understand, don't you? Those aren't just glib words. I've thought about you—about us—very hard.' He laughed shortly. 'In fact I've thought about little else all day.'

'Yes. You made it very clear you wanted to be alone. I shouldn't have come after you like that. It's my fault.'

'Fault.' He dismissed the word with a cut of his hand. 'That doesn't come into it. I don't mind telling you that I'm deeply surprised and flattered by your words. Back at the lodge you made me feel about as welcome as a plague of mosquitoes.'

'I was very rude. Especially when you came up to me in the bar. I had no right to speak to you like that. I wanted to apologise, but it never seemed the right moment.'

'I don't know. You had the perception to see that my intentions were entirely dishonourable. If you hadn't warned me away I'm afraid I might have made far more of a nuisance of myself than I did. If you can believe that!'

She smiled. Those first abrasive encounters seemed light-years ago. Since then Brent had come to fill her thoughts so completely that it was impossible to remember life before she had got to know him better.

He had no idea, she reflected. He thought she was attracted to him in the same way as he was to her. He had no idea how she really felt about him—but then, neither did she. She could not have put a name to the deep stirrings and confusions he aroused within her.

There was a long silence then, but a silence of close companionship. She was achingly aware of the man at her side, as they sat hip to hip, and she knew instinctively that it was the same for him. Tension ran between them like high-voltage wires. Yet, curiously, because it had been acknowledged, it did not matter. It simply felt right to be together like they were.

Brent picked up a stick and began to draw patterns in the dust at his feet. After a time he said, 'You know,

I still can't figure you out, Kate.'

'What do you mean?'

'You're one of the most mature, level-headed, perceptive women I've ever met. What I can't square in my mind is how you came to be involved with someone like Charlie's father, who sounds, from everything you said, to be a complete and utter disaster.'

'I was only eighteen,' she protested. 'I wasn't very mature then——'

'It still doesn't make sense to me.'

'Maybe you've got too flattering an impression of me.'

He shook his head slowly. 'This is going to sound big-headed, but I'm a good judge of human nature. I'm not often wrong about people.'

She paused for a long time before answering. Brent moved his foot to wipe away the patterns he had drawn, then began again. She knew he was not going to speak but was determined to draw her out. She opened her mouth, drew breath, then closed it again, her nerve failing.

'I can answer your questions,' she said finally, and as she did so she felt her heart begin a slow, anxious beat of pain. What she was about to tell him, she had never told anyone before. 'I've had a lot of years to figure it out for myself.'

She linked her hands around her knees, hugging herself to find the courage to go on. But she was tapping areas of deepest hurt and betrayal, and the words came out with tortured slowness.

'You know my parents were divorced?'

Brent nodded.

'It happened years ago, when I was quite small. I don't remember my father living at home, but I always adored him. He was my favourite person in the whole world. I just lived for the summer holidays when I would fly out to Africa to see him.'

Slowly she got into her stride. 'Everything about those trips was magical for me—getting off the aeroplane and hearing the cicadas, the smell of the frangipani, the sound of the rain on the tin roof of his bungalow. I used to lie awake and watch the geckoes on the walls of my bedroom and long to stay with him and never go back to Surrey.

'And every year he organised a safari for me—at least, I used to assume it was for me although when I look back now I'm not so sure. There was always a group of his friends, and we'd set off in a couple of ancient jeeps into the wilds, and my father would grow more and more cheerful the further we drove from civilisation.

'They were marvellous trips. My father knew everything there was to know about the bush. He could name every tree and every insect, and he never, ever fussed about boring things like bedtimes or whether the conversation was suitable for young ears.' She laughed freely, remembering. 'I learnt a lot about life sitting around campfires keeping my ears open! Looking back, I can see why my mother was always uneasy about those journeys. I used to think she was scared I'd be eaten by a lion, but I can see now it was the human element that bothered her more. My father's friends were a pretty strange bunch, drifters and loners. As for my father, she called him feckless, but I wouldn't hear a word against him. I idolised him!'

She turned, anxious to make herself understood.

'Can you see? All my friends' fathers worked in the City, or ran garages, or did something boring in insurance. They wore suits and came home at six o'clock every night. My father lived in Africa and could tell the difference between lion and cheetah spoor at a glance. I didn't see much of him, but at Christmas he would always send me something exotic and wonderful like an ivory bangle or a tribal spear. I kept a photograph of him on my dressing-table and wrote long schoolgirl's letters to him every week.'

'Did he write back?'

'No,' she said, quietly. It still hurt, the memory of the endless excuses she had to make up to herself for the airmail envelope that never fell through the letterbox. 'My mother was right. He was feckless. He lived for the moment, but when people were out of sight, they were out of mind.'

'What happened? Does he still live in Zambia?'

There was a lump the size of an egg swelling in her throat. She shook her head. Her voice, when it came, was squeezed thin by the need to hold back tears.

'He'd said that when I was seventeen, the summer I left school, we'd go on an extra special trip, a really long one, right up through Tanzania to the coast. I thought about it all through my examinations. It was what kept me going. I couldn't think why he hadn't written to send me my plane ticket. June came, then July, and there was still no word. I wrote to him, but he didn't reply, and then I tried to get through on the telephone——' She faltered. Brent glanced at her, concerned. 'They said the line was no longer in use. Three weeks later a letter came. It was an airmail letter, but not from Zambia. From Singapore.' She paused again.

'From your father?'

'Yes. It wasn't very long, he was never much of a writer. He said he was sorry to let me down but his life had been in upheaval. He said he had got married again, to a Chinese nurse he had met in Lusaka, and they had decided to move to Malaysia, where her family came from. He was looking for a job and he would be in touch as soon as they settled down. There was a line about how I must go out and see them as soon as possible, and the wonderful trips we could go on—but I knew he didn't mean it, and I was right. Neither I nor my mother ever heard from him again.'

'He just abandoned you totally?' Brent's voice sounded shocked.

Perversely she felt the need to protect her childhood idol. 'I'm sure he meant to get in touch. Maybe life was difficult for them, or it took a long time to settle and by the time he got round to writing again he was embarrassed at his long silence. And he knew I was virtually grown up. He'd done his bit for me in my childhood years.' She stared reflectively at her feet. 'He was a humble man. I honestly think he thought he'd forfeited any rights to a proper relationship with me when he got divorced. I don't think he ever realised just what he meant to me.' She tried to bring her father's face to mind, but it was a distressingly blurred and faded image. She drew her breath in sharply, like a sob.

Brent said, 'Kate?'

'I'm all right.'

'So after that?'

'After that, what do you think?' she said, harshly. 'The man I loved most in the whole world had just turned his back and vanished. That was what men were like, so why trust any of them? John—Charlie's father—was no better and no worse than any of the others. I didn't have any plans, any expectations of life any more, so it was easy enough just to drift into a relationship that everyone else seemed pleased about.'

There was a long silence.

'I was right last night,' Brent said finally. 'You were punishing yourself. But I got the wrong reason. You decided that your father didn't love you, so you must be unlovable, so you'd get embroiled in a totally unsuitable relationship, thereby hurting him—and you.'

'Yes. No,' she said, confused. 'It was like that in a way. I think I knew at the back of my mind that it wouldn't ever work out. But what you're saying is too bald. It's never like that in real life, is it? You can't untangle things that clearly.'

'What would you have done if your father hadn't fled?'

'I don't know. I think at the back of my mind I always hoped the summer holiday would turn into an extended stay. I had daydreams about finding a job, and living with him in Zambia, at least for a time. My school wanted me to apply for a university place, but I wouldn't because I half hoped I wouldn't be around to take it up.'

She followed with her eyes the restless pattern of Brent's doodling stick. The pattern on the sand, clear in the light of the rising moon, was a complicated mesh of squares and triangles. 'Do you think I'm crazy?'

Brent scrubbed it out abruptly and threw down the stick, turning to her.

'No. I think you had a terrible knock, at an important stage in your life—and you took it as hard as you could.' His eyes scrutinised her face. 'Do you want to know what I think?'

She nodded slowly.

'I think you've got to start learning to trust people all over again. I think you've got to dare to take risks, make mistakes. I think you've got to stop giving yourself such a hard time and learn to enjoy yourself—for your sake and for Charlie's. You were never born to live like a nun.'

Her face was raised to his, close, questioning, her grey eyes meeting his dark gaze. She felt as if an enormous burden had been rolled from her shoulders. The relief of recounting her story was immeasurable. She smiled tremulously at him, her lips curving perfectly.

I just offered to come out of my nunnery,' she reminded him. 'The offer was rejected.'

He held her eyes before replying and she saw him draw in his breath sharply. He shook his head hard. 'Not me, Kate. Please. I'm not to be trusted. Don't make me hurt you.'

They were close, so close she could feel his breath

grazing her cheek. She dropped her gaze. The dark hairs on his arm were raised. Without thinking she covered them with her hand. 'You're cold!'

'Kate. Don't!'

'I wasn't——' She flushed, realising how her impulsive gesture must seem. 'I didn't mean to—I didn't think——'

She felt him tremble under her touch and withdrew her hands as if stung. But it was already too late. His hand were reaching out to her.

'I know. I know what you're saying.'

He was standing, raising her with him. 'Oh, if you hadn't touched me, I might have done it, I just might have resisted you! It's been hell sitting here, listening, hearing your pain. Not being able to hold you, touch you.'

His hands cupped her neck, ran down her shoulders, held her back close to him. She trembled. Even beneath the bulk of her two sweaters she could feel their bold, sensual pressure.

'Kate,' he said, and the low resonance of his voice pierced through to her heart. 'I want to kiss you so much.'

Then his lips found hers, kissing her again and again, like a man unable to slake his thirst, tearing himself away only to search her eyes before sinking his mouth again.

'Oh,' he groaned, shifting his weight to draw her more closely to him, not masking the desire he felt for her as his hands went up beneath her sweaters to find the swells and curves of her body in its thin cotton shirt.

'All I've thought about all day is you, holding you like this!' Again his lips sank, to her hair, her ear, the slenderness of her neck, and to her lips again, to part them and take the sweetness of her mouth in a kiss that seemed as wide as an ocean and as long as time.

She held him tighter, no longer ashamed of the hunger she felt for him. There were no secrets any more, and no deceptions. They were man and woman, together, pleasing each other, and the future would take care of itself.

Tall against him, their legs entwined as their bodies found their fit, her fingers locked in his hair, and she pulled his mouth down to hers, willing their closeness never to end.

CHAPTER EIGHT

SPLASH went Charlie, diving into the pool. Splash. Splash. Splash.

With every dive water sprayed over her legs and book. She moved back, but he only seemed to dive higher and more roughly, so the cold drops still splattered her heated skin.

'Charlie, for goodness' sake! Can't you do that somewhere else?' There was a sharp edge to her voice that made him obey her without the usual protests and questions.

She should not be so irritable, she knew, but ever since they had returned to the lodge she had felt restless and miserable, unable to settle to anything. In only a few days, she thought, they would be back in London, and she no longer knew whether to feel glad or sorry.

Of course, there was a quite obvious reason for her short temper, she knew. For years she had lived in a happy cocoon of celibacy, glad to be free of the danger of hurt and disappointment that being part of a couple brought.

But Brent had changed all that. His arms about her had roused her body, reawakening its needs and urgent wantings. Her skin felt tender and super-sensitive, her limbs restless.

Her thoughts by day were wayward, and by night

she blushed at the directions they took as she lay, sleepless, in the darkness. Sometimes she fingered her lips, trying to remember the exact feeling of his mouth covering hers.

But already it was a fading, elusive memory. Brent had gone to ground. She had seen nothing of him in the two days since they returned and she knew he was avoiding her. Maybe he had even left, she thought suddenly, and the idea struck a chill in her heart. It was impossible to think she would never see him again, but at the same time it was all too easily possible. If he chose to take the easy way out, he could disappear to Nairobi without trace.

But out of what, exactly? Two embraces hardly added up to a relationship, let alone anything lasting. To him it could simply be a passing fancy, a sexual attraction which, for many good and worthy reasons, he chose not to pursue. With his constant travels and adventures such encounters must be commonplace.

What to her had become an obsession was probably to him a mere distraction, already put out of sight and out of mind. After all, he had told her he wasn't to be trusted. It wasn't his fault that she had chosen not to listen.

A group of people came through the bushes carrying towels. She scanned them anxiously, but the tanned and lithe figure she hoped to see was not among them.

The lodge was filling up now. The quiet intimacy of their first few days there had evaporated. She barely saw Mike or Sandy now, and when she did it was only for a snatched few words as they rushed from job to job.

Yet just as she thought that, Sandy appeared, as if conjured to reality out of her thoughts.

'Kate, I thought I'd find you here. There's a couple of things I wanted to ask you.' She crouched down next to the sun-lounger, obviously in too much of a hurry to stay. 'Mike's got to run the boys back to school this evening. We got the all-clear this afternoon. They were moaning about having to leave Charlie, so Mike wondered if you'd let him drive down to Nairobi with them all. It would give him the chance to see a bit more of the country—I'm sure he'd enjoy it.'

'I think he'd love to.'

'But he'd have to stay in town overnight. Mike never drives back here in the dark unless he has to—not since he ran slap into a huge herd of wildebeest. He stays at Brent's house.' She laughed. 'We always use it. We call it our town house.'

'Oh, I don't know.' She frowned. Charlie was so precious to her it made her feel anxious when he was away at nights. But she crushed down her over-protective instincts. 'Will Brent be there?'

'No. Why?' Sandy looked puzzled. 'He's still here. Surely you've seen him around.'

'No. I think he must be avoiding me.' She tried to laugh lightly, but it sounded tinny and false.

'Oh,' said Sandy. Then 'Oh,' again, in a voice that told her she understood too much for comfort. No doubt Mike had told her what he had seen and sensed on their trip and, although she was sure the night had cloaked their embraces in darkness, he would have had to be blind not to see the attraction and tension between them.

She quickly scanned Sandy's face and what she saw there disturbed her. There seemed to be sympathy there, but also something else. Was it a trace of pity?

'I'm sure Mike will take good care of Charlie. I don't see why he can't go,' she said quickly.

'Good. That leads me on to the other thing—since we'll both be on our own this evening I wondered if you would come and have supper with me. Not in the lodge, at home.'

'That would be lovely!'

'You know where it is, don't you? The white house across the lawn from the pool. Follow the lighted path and you can't go wrong—it leads to our front door.'

'You won't go to any trouble, will you? I know how busy you've been with the season getting under way.'

'Don't worry, I'm spoilt to death. My cook will rustle up something for us.' Sandy stood up. 'I'd better get on. There's a big party arriving later and three of the waiters have had to go off to a funeral. I'll see you about eight. Have a nice afternoon.'

Kate's room seemed strangely silent that evening, with Charlie gone in a flurry of shouted farewells and a whirl of dust from the Land Rover, but once she had adjusted to the eerie quiet she found she was enjoying the unaccustomed solitude.

She stepped out of her clothes in the bedroom, able for once to go naked, caught sight of herself in the mirror and was astonished at what she saw.

Her skin was lightly tanned from a week of African sun, and regular swimming had tautened her slender figure. Her height was balanced by full breasts and set off by long shapely legs.

She stroked her hand down her throat, grey eyes meeting grey eyes in the mirror, and saw with genuine surprise that she looked very good indeed. The only flaw she could find was a small line of anxiety that marked the centre of her brow with shadow. She pressed a finger along it to smooth it clear.

Lonely. Bitter. Brent's words came back to her like a tolling bell. In a very few years that mark would be permanent. Then would come the others, crow's feet around the eyes, furrows on the forehead.

She ran her hands down her sides, feeling the skin soft and perfect. This was the body that was beating out its needs so urgently in her brain, the body that was demanding Brent's arms around it again, his lips on hers. It tightened and melted even as she thought of him and, suddenly embarrassed at her unaccustomed self-regard, she turned abruptly away and went to the bathroom.

Yet no matter how hard she tried, she could not put the thought of him from her mind, although Sandy's companionship proved a help, and her entrancing house provided some distraction.

'It's lovely, Sandy, It's straight out of Hemingway or something.'

'I sometimes think we've gone overboard on the Africana,' Sandy said critically, looking around at the skins and carvings that adorned the white walls, 'but each of these things means something special to us. They're not just tourist tat.'

'I think it's just right. It all fits in with the surroundings. It wouldn't look right any other way. I mean, you couldn't have English chintz or art deco or anything like that. Not with cheetahs padding past your front door!'

They were sitting on the veranda, drinking chilled white wine and listening to a Mozart quartet. Sandy was darning a sweater of Mike's as they talked, and the homely sight gave Kate a searing pang of jealousy.

Everything about the house, from the photographs of the boys on the piano to the comfortable scatter of books and binoculars on the table, spoke of a loving family. She had never before envied anyone their domestic life, but in this African home she saw a sudden vision of the kind of life she yearned for.

'This must seem a million miles from London,' said Sandy as the cicadas got into full voice.

'Thank goodness for that,' Kate said with feeling. 'I know which life I'd rather have.'

'A lot of people say that to me, but they only see the good side. They don't think about what it's like to have water rationed down to a washing-up bowl a day, or to wake up and find your whole vegetable garden has been wrecked by elephant in the night.'

'I know. Don't forget I've spent a lot of time in Africa.'

'But your life must be so—oh, I don't know, sophisticated, I suppose. I mean, look at you.' Sandy gestured at Kate's black jersey dress and elegant gold choker. 'I normally only see things like that in old copies of Vogue that the visitors leave behind. It's all I can do not to get up and examine every last stitch.'

Kate smiled. 'You'll probably hit me if I say, "Oh, this old thing" but it's true. I've had this dress five years. I wear it everywhere because it doesn't crease and it never seems to date. The choker——' she fingered it '——was a present to myself when I landed my last promotion.'

'It looks like the sort of little trinket I imagine the men in your life giving you,' Sandy said with a wicked grin. 'I can just see them, tall, dark and handsome, driving up in their white Porsches to sweep you off to dinner at Claridge's——'

Kate grimaced. 'They don't exist, except in magazine stories. Anyway, I'd much rather buy my own treats; that way I don't have to feel grateful to anyone.' She sipped her wine. 'The only man in my life is Charlie.'

Even as she spoke she knew it was no longer true. For better or worse, Brent was in her life now. She had tried to put him from her mind, but she had failed, completely and utterly. Like a love-struck teenager, she was a helpless victim of her own fantasies and longings.

Sandy said, 'That kind of self-sufficiency is usually the greatest turn-on of all. I'm sure you have men queuing round the block.'

'I'm not short of offers,' she admitted, 'but none of them interest me. I've got rather used to running my own show, and I'm not particularly keen on handing over the reins to anyone else.'

Sandy said casually, 'You know, you often sound just like Brent. You're each as self-sufficient as the other.'

Kate looked up sharply and caught Sandy's eye. She dumped her darning down in her lap and grinned sheepishly. 'All right, I'm not very good at being devious. Brent made no secret about how much you had caught his eye. In fact Mike and I had a rather tedious few hours with him the other night when he could talk of little else. He twisted Mike's arm to invite you along on the trip——'

'That was Brent's idea?'

'Well, Mike thought it was a good one,' Sandy said hastily. 'He knew how much the boys were enjoying Charlie's company and he guessed from what you'd said about your bush trips that you would be an asset in camp. Anyone who can rustle up bacon and eggs on an open fire is more than welcome.'

She drank from her glass, thoughts churning, as Sandy said, 'I'll be honest, I wasn't wild about the idea. I've known Brent long enough to know he's bad news for any woman who takes him too seriously. He's a law unto himself, and he's never seen the attraction of stability or,' she paused, almost imperceptibly, 'faithfulness. Why, he was best man at our wedding and he spent the night before trying to persuade Mike he was making a grave mistake. It took me a long time for me to forgive him that—and just as long for him to acknowledge he was wrong.'

'You needn't have worried——' Kate paused, then saw no reason to mask the truth, or at least part of it. 'He *is* a very attractive man, I can't pretend otherwise. I intended to resist his charms but in the end I didn't quite make it, especially after he saved Charlie from that rhino. Even so, two kisses hardly constitute a recipe for disaster, and since we'll soon be going our separate ways it hardly matters one way or another.'

'From what you said this afternoon it looks as if he's

decided to drop the chase. Knowing Brent—and the way he was raving about you earlier—I'd say it was the best compliment he could pay you.'

She shrugged. 'I'll have to take your word for that. It doesn't feel very nice to be dropped flat like this, even if it is for my own emotional health. I must say I'd rather make my own decisions in that area.'

'Better to be hurt a bit now, than a lot later,' Sandy said bluntly. Then she looked up and added emphatically, 'And all Brent's girlfriends do get hurt in the end, believe me, Kate.'

'Oh, I do. I do. And,' she raised her chin and lied valiantly, 'it's only my pride that's taken a bit of a knock, nothing worse. I can see he's always been a wanderer, a loner. In fact I find it hard to picture him as a farmer, rooted to one spot, don't you?'

'Oh, I don't know, I can see him doing anything he sets his mind on. The only thing I really can't ever see him doing is losing his head, or his heart, over a woman.' She put down her glass and seeing Kate's face said, 'This is awfully gloomy talk—let's go and eat and discuss something more cheerful. After all, we've both got a rare night off—we're supposed to be enjoying ourselves.'

And they did, somewhat to Kate's surprise, although it was still early when Sandy's discreet yawns told her it was time to go. She kissed her new friend warmly on the cheek.

'Thank you, Sandy, it's been lovely.' And it had. Good food and wine, and the chance to swap notes on the trials and joys of raising young boys had made the evening fly past, and had even pushed that uncomfortable conversation about Brent from the forefront of her thoughts.

But it flooded back to her as soon as she set off into the night. Sandy had offered to walk her back, but she protested that she was quite safe and unworried. 'I'll enjoy the walk,' she had insisted. 'It will clear my head.'

But it didn't. Just the opposite, in fact, since the moment the night engulfed her, troubled thoughts rose up to swamp all reason from her brain.

Brent, drummed her feet on the pathway. Brent. Brent. Brent.

Sandy's disclosure that it was he who persuaded Mike to ask her along on the trip had come as a shock, and part of her felt angry that he could manipulate her so readily.

If she hadn't spent those few days with him, if their only contact had been the occasional meeting in and around the lodge, then she might have resisted his charms. But their enforced intimacy had so broken down her resistance that she now felt half crazed with desire for him.

Swirling thoughts of him, his arms around her, her hands in his hair, carried her in a daze back to her room.

She banged the door shut as if to leave her demons outside, and leant against it, breathing heavily. Charlie's bed was starkly empty, the white sheet pulled tight across it. She stared at it bleakly. He was all she had in life and his absence made everything seem cold and hollow.

She turned about. The room seemed to ring with a

silence that mocked her, and her controlled and shuttered life. Empty, it said. Loveless. Cold.

'Oh!' She felt she was choking on the emotions that battled inside her. Her longing to see Brent was overwhelming, her need of him too powerful to resist. She crossed her arms and hugged herself tightly, feeling tension coiled like a spring in every muscle beneath the thin material of her dress. The walls of the room seemed to be coming closer, squeezing in on her, crushing the breath from her lungs.

She went to the door and flung it open, needing air to breathe. Outside the moon hung low in the sky like a polished silver medal, framed by the black branches of the jacaranda trees.

The cicadas sang and throbbed in a shrieking chorus that echoed the hot pulsing of her brain. The night air cooled her skin, but not her thoughts. Somewhere, not far away, was Brent——.

And suddenly her feet were running, running, carrying her in search of him, although for what purpose she could not tell.

'Oh!'

She cried out fear and shock as she cannonned headlong into a black, unyielding mass. There was a muffled exclamation.

'Kate!'

His arms came up to steady her. Her own hands touched his shoulders.

'Oh, Kate,' he repeated hoarsely and his arms tightened about her until the scent of his skin filled her nostrils and she felt her body melt and yield to their pressure.

Then his lips were seeking hers, kissing her with such pent-up passion that she was engulfed in his fire. 'Oh,' he groaned again, as his lips sank deeper and her mouth opened to his, and they were holding each other like two desperate drowners.

Any last lingering doubts were stripped from her as she felt the force of his urgent need and their lips strained together in a savage quest for fulfilment.

'I thought you had gone,' she gasped, as she buried her head in his shoulder, exulting at the rightness of being enfolded by him again.

He spoke against her hair. 'I was trying to do the right thing, Kate—for once in my life. Trying to keep away from you. It's been hell. I'd just lost the battle. I was coming to find you.'

'I was looking for you!' she exclaimed. 'I was going to the bar. At least I think I was. I'm not sure exactly what I was doing! I seemed to have lost all reason!'

He laughed, low and short, and the rough sound of his voice at her ear made her quiver inside.

Then he kissed her again, long and hard and skilfully, taking possession of her with a new certainty.

'Come on,' he said, holding her close, and she did not ask where they were going because she did not care. The feeling of his arm around her shoulders was destination enough.

He led her to his room, shutting the door behind them. When the light went on she saw orderly piles of papers and books on a desk beside a portable work-processor. His clothes were less tidy. Jeans and a shirt were thrown carelessly across the bed.

He saw her eyes on the bed and read the sudden

apprehension in them.

'Do you want a drink?'

She nodded, suddenly shy, wishing they were still out in the darkness of the night. She caught his eye, looking away, caught his gaze again and felt colour tingeing her cheeks.

'I'm out of practice at this sort of thing,' she confessed, half laughing to cover her confusion.

Brent did not laugh. His face seemed hardened by emotion. He stepped back to her, and held her close in his arms.

'Thank God for that,' he said, with such deliberate intensity her eyes widened on his, and he scoured her face as if he would commit every last detail to memory for ever.

She looked at him, the face that was now so familiar and yet still so unknown, the tawny gaze, now darkened, the sensual lips and the straight planes of his jaw, and she felt her heart beating an uneven tattoo of desire.

And what she felt must have shown in the way her lips softened and parted, because she saw him swallow and then he was finding her mouth again, softly and seekingly, taking his time to know her while his hands held her shoulders without moving, as if he were holding something that was precious to him.

It was she who moved in the embrace, roused by his lips and needing to pull him closer, but he resisted the pressure of her hands on his back.

'What do you want?' he asked her huskily.

'What do you mean?'

They had both pulled back to see each other and

their words were hesitant and slow.

'I don't want you to do anything you don't want to.'

She looked into the straight depths of his gaze, thought of her lonely room and rejected the thought instantly.

'I can't leave,' she confessed. 'Not now.'

He regarded her slowly. 'There mustn't be any misunderstandings. I want to be honest with you, Kate.'

She looked at him, knowing he was going to say what she would much prefer unsaid.

'There aren't,' she said hastily. 'You already have—been honest. I'm under no illusions.'

He still looked hard at her. She thought he might push her away, and she knew she could not bear it.

She shook her head. 'You don't make it easy——'

'I don't want it to be easy. I don't want you to wake up tomorrow groaning with regret at what you've done. I don't want to sweep you off your feet, or make you lose your head, or any of the other euphemisms people employ when they want to opt out of responsibility for their actions.'

'I made my decision when I came to seek you out. I didn't expect you to offer me a cup of cocoa.'

Laughter made his mouth crook and his eyes wrinkle, and a wriggle of warmth stirred deep inside her at the look in them. Then his face grew serious.

'I want you to stay with me, Kate,' he said after a pause. 'I want to make love to you. I want it very, very much.' As he spoke he ran his hands up her arms to the warmth of her neck, lifting her hair and cupping her head before retracing her shoulders. She ached with desire for him, even as they stood barely touching.

His eyes held hers as his fingers moved to unbutton her dress and let it slither to the floor. She stepped out of it, kicking off her shoes. His hands moved to her back, to unclasp her bra and let her full breasts free, and then he slid his fingers lightly down over the sides of her pelvis to slide off the white wisp of lace that covered her hips.

She stood naked under his gaze, head up, her eyes on his. Although he had scarcely touched her, her breasts stiffened with longing to be caressed by him and her body pulsed with need.

He looked the length of her tall figure, full but slender, then back to her eyes. 'I knew you would be flawless,' he murmured, as his hands took her by the waist to pull her to him. 'You are my idea of the perfect woman.'

He kissed her again, his hands roaming the length of her back, cupping her buttocks to him until the beat of heat became a hot throbbing that diffused into every part of her.

She needed to feel his skin against hers and shrugged away his jacket to open his shirt and ease it off. He stroked her breasts as she did so, making them swell and tauten under the light pressure that was less of a caress than a promise of what was to come.

'It's not fair,' she whispered, smiling. 'I'm at a disadvantage.'

'Not for long,' he said and with one hand he tugged at the belt of his trousers, helping her to free him of his clothes.

Before, when she had seen him shirtless or in swimming-trunks, she had cast covert glances at his figure. Now she looked at him frankly, feasting her eyes on the wide shoulders and narrow hips clothed in lean, brown muscle.

'Now you see what you do to me,' he said with a wry glance at her. 'Can you imagine the agony I had to endure being so close to you yet not able to touch you or hold you?'

As he spoke he drew her to him so that they met length to length and the shock of that contact was so great that there was suddenly no more time for talking.

He pulled her to the bed and lay down with her, kissing her constantly as his hands caressed her breasts and the curves of her hips and thighs.

The enormity of her need for him was overwhelming. She had fastened the lid on her sexual nature so tightly that now it was freed it erupted into urgent, headlong life. Her hands felt the smooth skin of his back, the muscled legs, the wonderful warmth of him against her. Their legs were entwined and he shuddered as she touched the heart of his desire, groaning out her name. She moved beneath him, wanting him to cover her and join with her, impatient with need, her body hammering with desire.

He let his body fit to hers beneath him as he kissed her and roused her until she thought her head would explode. As if from a long distance she heard her voice calling his name, gasping a plea, and her hands moved to guide him to her, into her.

'Oh!'

Nothing had ever felt so right. She felt completed by

him, as if the final piece of the jigsaw that made her whole had at last fallen into place, and she held him as tightly as he embraced her.

But as she did so, his own control broke, and the storm of thrusting passion that engulfed them pushed aside all tenderness and restraint.

CHAPTER NINE

'MY GOD.' Brent finally raised his head from where he lay collapsed at her shoulder and levered himself on to his elbow. 'I needed you so much—I'm sorry for any lack of finesse.'

She shook her head. 'It was the same for me. You must have seen that.'

He stroked back the damp strands of her fringe, trailing his fingers down to tuck her hair behind her ears. The tender touch made her quiver and close her eyes, as sensual as a cat. She felt wonderful, relaxed and sated. She stretched her long limbs on the cool sheets.

He nodded, amused. 'I'd say you were a lady who, once she makes up her mind, likes to get on with the matter in hand.' Then he searched her eyes. 'It's been a long time.'

It was a statement, not a question.

'Yes. Years,' she acknowledged. 'Since every relationship I embarked on turned out to be an utter disaster, I decided it was simply easier to cut that side of things out of my life altogether.'

A shadow seemed to darken his eyes.

'Then why me?'

'I——' She felt unsure what words to choose. 'You got through my defences——' It was an evasion. As she looked at him lying next to her, staring down into her eyes, as she felt the exquisite tender caresses of his fingers on her bare shoulders and arm, she knew exactly why.

She loved him. She loved him completely and utterly and hopelessly.

She closed her eyes. She wanted to be with him always, to build a life together, to grow old with him. Ruthlessly she pushed such thoughts away.

All she had was tonight, this one moment, and she wanted to savour every second. She would deal with the pain later, when she had to.

'And it won't be,' he paused, feeling for her words, 'an "utter disaster"?'

'It can't be, can it? It's not a relationship. It's a holiday romance, a one-night stand.'

Her words came out more harsh and emphatic than she intended. He flung himself back on his pillow. She held her breath, hoping against forlorn hope for a contradication, but he only sighed.

For a moment there was bleakness between them, but then he turned to her, and gathering her to him, kissed her deeply and tenderly, warming away the bad thoughts with his closeness. She abandoned herself to him, wrapped round by the smell of his skin and the feel of his lips.

'Let me see you.' He pushed the sheet down from her shoulders and regarded her slim body, running his hand down her side from shoulder to hip. 'You're perfect in every way,' he murmured. 'Just perfect.' He touched her breast with his hand, running the ball of his thumb lightly over her nipple, and she shivered at the sensuality of his touch.

'There's something so special about you, Kate,' he said, still lightly caressing her skin. 'Ever since I first saw you I haven't been able to get you out of my mind. At first I thought it was just because you were a beautiful woman, with that glossy hair of yours and those disturbingly direct eyes. I wanted to stare and stare at you until I'd committed every detail of you to memory.

'But it's more than that. There's an elusive quality about you that drives me crazy. You're tough and self-sufficient, but you're also so vulnerable and defensive, and it's impossible to say where the one ends and the other begins. I feel all the time that you're hiding something—the essence of you, if you like—protecting it close, as you would a baby.'

She gestured at herself. 'I'm hardly hiding anything now.' But she knew it was a lie. She was hiding something, hiding her love from him, cupping it close to her and praying he would not see the depth of her need for him.

He said, 'I suppose I was foolish enough to think that if we went to bed, if I knew you in the Biblical sense, then it would let me know you in other ways. A typical male arrogance, if you like.'

'I hardly know you, either,' she pointed out. 'I know almost nothing about you.' But the kind of details she meant seemed immaterial. As she looked at him, lying in such intimacy with her, she knew she met him on a level where such things had no importance.

'I'll tell you anything you want to know,' he offered, but she shook her head emphatically. More knowledge would only bring more pain.

'All this——' She gestured at the two of them together. 'It's just for now, just for tonight. Let's not complicate it more than we need to.'

He looked at her, long and dark, and she had a curious sensation that behind his gaze his thoughts were spinning rapidly away on complex calculations that she could not begin to guess at. Then he came back to her, his eyes warming.

'Maybe. But if that's the case,' he said softly, 'let's make the most of it.'

This time there was no urgency of desperation. He kissed her mouth, her eyes, her ears, and trailed his lips down to the tender hollows of her shoulders before finding the sensitive tips of ears to moisten and rouse.

She bit back a groan at the spirals of sensation that began to wind through her body and moved to seek his lips, to offer him the same pleasure he was giving her.

'No, Kate,' he whispered against her neck. 'Let go for once, really let go. You don't have to do anything. This is all for you. I'm in charge now.'

And he was, learning her body with his eyes and his mouth and his hands, while she sank down into a sea of exquisite sensation that banished all dark thoughts from the room.

It was, she thought, like shrugging off layer after layer of heavy clothes, as his lips found her soft underarms and then moved to explore each full, dark nipple.

She tensed as his lips moved down over her stomach, but he said, 'Trust me,' and she did, yielding up her body to him and letting her arms spread, open and relaxed on the bed.

Now the feelings he was conjuring in her were a kaleidoscope of shuddering sensations. His fingers lightly stroked her legs, the soft inner thighs, heating her desire until her breasts pressed hard against his chest and she longed for the fulfilment that his body, hard against her, promised.

She reached for him, but he pinned her wrists with his hands, as he found her lips with his, commanding her again to relax and put her trust in him.

And she marvelled at how exactly he knew where she needed his touch and his lips, and when the feelings he was conjuring to life became almost too intense to bear, as he explored every inch of her and brought her whole body to a quivering pitch of need that only union with him would assuage.

Only then did he move to take her, kissing her deeply, almost reverently, as he slowly began to move inside her, making certain that she matched his ascent to the place where no more pleasure was possible beyond the final, tumbling fulfilment that was unlike anything she had ever known before in its almost unbearable intensity.

'Oh,' she groaned, in her tumult, 'how I love you!' but the words were masked by her gasping breaths and his deep sounds of pleasure.

Sleep fell lightly upon them both until some sound outside in the bush disturbed them. She listened to a hyena call, then looked at her watch. It was one o'clock. Brent, beside her, was like a Greek sculpture, with the single sheet thrown over his lean limbs. Her body still felt sated and washed with pleasure, and all tension had fled from her. Without opening his eyes Brent closed his hand hard over her wrist.

'Forget the time. I've no intention of letting you go.'

He pulled her down beside him, holding her close in his arms until she slept, and she woke again only when it was morning and light was flooding past the curtains into the white-walled room.

She looked at Brent, his breath coming easily as he slept in peace beside her, and was swamped with her love for him.

Her hand stroked his shoulder, then moved down beneath the sheet, along the length of his brown back.

'What——'

He began to wake from sleep, rolling over on to his back. Without thought she leant across him, her hair brushing his chest as she found his lips and kissed him deeply, not masking her feelings. His eyes opened fractionally, sensuously, so that she could see a glint of white and tawny brown.

'Oh,' he groaned, smiling, 'what a perfect way to start the day,' and he captured her with his arms and pulled her down on top of him, allowing her this time to return some small fraction of the pleasure he had bestowed on her last night.

Afterwards she closed her eyes and thought about their lovemaking. In just one night they had explored more moods and sensations than she had ever guessed were possible. If only they could stay together, then she knew it would be a rich and precious dimension of their lives. But they could not, and it would not. Their time together was up. Her eyes squeezed tight shut. Now the pain was about to start.

She got out of bed and went quickly to the bathroom, gathering her clothes as she went. When she returned she was dressed and had masked her face with a cool resolution she did not feel.

Brent, still in bed, looked surprised at her appearance, then angry.

'I don't understand—what's the hurry?'

Don't you? she pleaded silently. Don't you see that I have to get out of here before the pain of loving you so hopelessly becomes impossible to bear?

'I need to get back. I've no idea when Charlie will be home.'

'They won't be back for hours. I was going to send for breakfast.'

'No!' She did not want anyone to see them together, not even a waiter.

'What are you going to do this morning? I thought we could borrow a Land Rover and drive out to the waterhole.'

She turned to him, almost savage. 'I don't think we should spend any more time together——'

'But you can't just walk out of here——'

'Why not? Men do it all the time.' The pain was beginning now, a raw aching hurt that made her want to nurse her side and cry. It cloaked her words with a venomous savagery.

'Yes,' he said shortly, 'and you know from bitter experience just how much it can hurt.'

Her eyes flickered on him uncertainly. What was he saying? That she could hurt him? It seemed unlikely.

'There's no future for us, Brent,' she said, more softly. 'And once Charlie's back, I can't spend time with you. I don't want him to know about this.'

She looked at him, longing for him to contradict her, but he only nodded slowly.

'I suppose I understand that.' His eyes held hers and there was an expression in them that she could not read. 'When do you leave?' he asked at last.

'In two days.'

He sighed. 'This is impossible——' he burst out angrily. 'I'll see you again.'

She thought of the lodge, and how impossible it would be for her and Charlie to hide away for two whole days. 'Yes. But——' He cocked an eye at her. She thought about Mike and Sandy. 'I—I don't want anyone to know about—what's happened.'

'You're ashamed?' His voice hardened.

'No, it's not that.' She spread her hands. 'It's private. It was just a moment in both our lives. If people know—' she hesitated, searching for the right words '—it'll become more than it is. They'll discuss us, and speculate——' and no doubt feel a pitying contempt for me, she added silently.

'So now it's over?' The hardness was still there.

His anger kindled hers. 'Of course it is!' she shouted. 'There's no other way, is there? It's how it has to be! Don't forget you spent a lot of time pointing out exactly that to me last night!' And she turned and slammed out.

Tears began to blind her as she hurried towards the shelter of her room, but not before she caught sight of Sandy coming down the path towards her.

As she dived for her room she saw Sandy falter and halt, taking in the hastening figure in its black dress and gold choker. She saw surprise on her face, and then something worse: the hateful, horrible pity that she had glimpsed there before.

CHAPTER TEN

THE Land Rover returned at lunch time, disgorging two dust-stained but cheerful passengers.

'My, Kate, your night off has obviously done you the world of good! I'll have to take Charlie away more often,' said Mike, patting her arm affectionately.

She flushed with embarrassment. She knew exactly what he meant, for although her thoughts were tormented, the body she inhabited today was the flesh and blood of a stranger. It had been caressed and loved into new life, and it showed in her every movement, newly graceful and free. Her skin glowed and her hair swung gleaming about her shoulders. It was as if the very air around her were charged with the vibrations of remembered love, and she felt sure people only had to glance at her to know what had wrought such dramatic changes in her.

She knew now that, at twenty-eight, she had been living the life of a girl, afraid of men and even more afraid of her own desires. Repression had made her sharp-tongued and defensive, so much so that even the way she walked had reflected this reined-in tension.

But this new knowledge was worthless to her, because without Brent the only option open to her was a solitary life, and in just two days' time the two of them would be a world apart, separated by continents.

She doubted if he would give her more than a passing thought.

'Thank you,' she got out. 'Did you have a good journey?'

Charlie tumbled out of the vehicle. 'It was great, Mum, terrific! We saw loads of giraffe on the way there, and their school is fabulous! They've got tons of playing fields, and they do games every afternoon, and—do you know what—in the holidays they have school safaris. Last year they went to Lake Rudolf and this year they're taking a dhow, a real Arab dhow, to Lamu. That's an island off the coast——' She hugged him hard, temporarily stemming the tide of excited words.

'Hold on, one thing at a time. I want to hear all about it, but in proper order. Let's get you washed and then we'll go and have some lunch.'

She had never seen Charlie so full of life, she thought, as he related his adventures between giant mouthfuls of steak. It was as if a curtain had been lifted for him on a perfect existence, a world of colour and freedom and light, far away from the cramped flat and grey asphalt playgrounds that marked the perimeter of his London world.

Her eyes felt heavy with her private loss and sadness, but she struggled to mask it, as she let him chatter on about all the things he had seen.

'Would you really like to go to a school like that?' she asked him. 'After all, Adam and Joe are boarders. They can't go home every night as you do.' She saw him hesitate, torn between honesty and loyalty. Honesty won.

'I don't think I'd mind, because you'd have all your friends there. Some of the boys stay from Monday to Friday and go home at weekends. I think I'd like that best. And it would be good for you, too——' he pointed out, logically. 'You could go out at nights, and things, and not have to worry about me all the time.'

She laughed. 'I like worrying about you—and I don't want to go out at nights. I'm far too tired!'

'Mike let me have a go at driving the Land Rover on the way down. I did about half a mile in the park, before we got on to the road. He said I was a natural! Joe and Adam did some as well.'

'My goodness! What was Nairobi like?'

He considered. 'It's very big, but it's not like London. There's lots of parks and trees and flowers. We had a meal at a café, outside on the pavement. Mike knows lots of people. They all kept coming up and saying hello. Then he took me to a museum, Oh——' He fished in his pocket and produced a tissue-wrapped parcel. 'That's for you. I thought you might be a bit fed up, being on your own.'

'For me? That's lovely. But you shouldn't have worried. I had supper with Sandy.'

She unwrapped her parcel. In her hand lay a tiny polished stone egg.

'I don't know what the stone is, but it's something semi-precious.'

'It's very precious to me,' she said, curling it in her hands. She had Charlie, her beautiful son Charlie. Why couldn't she be satisfied with that? But she couldn't, not any longer. Her hunger for Brent was like a huge weeping wound inside her.

All the time she talked to Charlie her thoughts were pulled back to him, and she was constantly on edge, expecting to see him appear on the terrace at any moment.

She wondered, with forlorn hope, whether he felt at all as she did, this morning. If he was experiencing even a hundredth, or a thousandth of the loss she carried inside her, then he would have to do something about it. Although what that could possibly be, she had no idea. Their lives were so far apart, and he had never pretended he was interested in anything but a brief affair.

'Brent's got masses of them at his house. About a hundred, all in a black wooden bowl.'

'Brent?' She jumped at his name, then frowned. She wouldn't have thought he was the sort of man who collected things like that.

'Mike said they're worth a fortune.'

'Oh.' She paused, then curiosity got the better of her. 'Is it a nice house?'

'Uh huh.' Charlie, at ten, wasn't very interested in houses. 'It's all sort of white and there's a maid who makes breakfast. Brent's got a computer, and a telex in his office. Mike wouldn't let me touch them, not even to try.' He laughed. 'Sarah said it was like living in a newspaper office. The telex is always starting up in the middle of the night!'

'Sarah?'

Her eyes slid like lasers to her son's innocent, happy face.

'Who's Sarah?'

He looked at her as if she were daft. 'It's her house.

Hers and Brent's. She's his wife.'

She had read in books of people in shock seeing
black mists swirling across their vision. Now she knew
it was true. She could barely see Charlie's face through
the whirling fog of darkness.

'Mum, what's the matter? Are you all right?'

She stood up, groping for the back of her chair.

'I think I ate something funny—I must just—stay
there——'

Somehow she found the shelter of the cloakroom
and managed to lock the door behind her before she
was violently sick. She stayed where she was long after
the spasm of shock had passed, pressing her forehead
to the cool wall, until the worst of the shaking had
subsided. Then she went out and methodically rinsed
her mouth and splashed her face with water.

She would not think, she thought, she would not let
herself think until later, and all the years of rigid self-
discipline stood her in good stead as she made her way
back to the table with only the pallor beneath her tan
bearing witness to her distress.

Charlie was tucking into raspberry cheesecake and
the sight made her stomach heave in protest. 'It must
have been those prawns,' he said, matter-of-factly.

'Yes. I'm all right now. Go on—you were telling me
about Sarah.'

It was like probing a throbbing tooth, you knew it
would hurt, but you could not stop yourself.

'She's nice——' He couldn't think of anything else
to say.

'Nice,' she said sharply, 'what sort of description is
that? Is she thin, fat, short, tall, blonde, dark? Does

she wear skirts or trousers—or maybe a rubber wetsuit and snorkel mask?'

He snorted his laughter, and she was relieved to see her feeble joke had masked the worst of her unreasonable anger.

'Um. She's sort of mediumish, blondish, and she wears those things that you sometimes wear. Like dungarees, only with tops like jackets.'

'Flying suits.'

'Yes. She wears those. In black, with a white T-shirt underneath.' Charlie was pleased with his observations. 'Oh, and she paints.'

'Paints?'

'Yes, she's got this huge studio at the back of the house where she works. She paints animals, elephants and things like that. They're really good. They're so real you think they're going to come out at you. Mike said she has exhibitions all over the place, America and Australia and everywhere.'

'Well, you have had an exciting time.' Her voice sounded thin and sour and she despised herself almost as much as she hated Brent. 'Charlie, I'm really not feeling very well. I think I'd better lie down this afternoon. Why don't you have a swim?'

'OK.'

An hour later there was a sharp rap on her door. 'Kate.' Brent's voice, peremptory, came through the wood into her darkened room.

She didn't answer. Misery had made her so wretched that she hardly had the energy to lift her head from the bed.

'Kate, for goodness' sake. I know you're there.

Charlie told me.'

There was a rattling of the knob.

'Go away,' she got out.

'This is ridiculous! We have to talk!'

'I don't want to talk to you. I don't want to see you.'

'What the hell has got into you?'

'How can you even ask me that!'

She pulled a pillow over her head and after a time he gave up and went away, his steps muted on the sandy path.

So she had been duped again, she thought wretchedly. Oh, she had had no real illusions about the long-term prospects for their relationship, despite her intermittent hope of some miracle. Brent had made sure of that and at the time she had almost welcomed what she thought was his ruthless honesty. But now she knew it wasn't honesty at all, just a different kind of lying.

She had thought he was different, but he wasn't. He was a man who lied and cheated on his wife. He was exactly like all the other men who had passed through her life—weak and heedless of anything except his own pleasure.

Flashes of memory came back to her like fragments of a bad dream.

She heard Brent's voice, low and rough, saying 'Trust me,' and she remembered how she had been fool enough to think she could. And she remembered Sandy's muted warning as they sat together on the veranda of her house. Brent, Sandy had told her, was not noted for his faithfulness. She must have picked that word quite deliberately, yet she had chosen to ignore its implications.

No wonder Sandy had looked at her with such pity as she fled this morning from Brent's room.

That memory made her sit up, suddenly shot through with anger. Sandy hadn't been honest with her, either. After all, she could have easily told her the whole wretched truth, without relying on dark hints and hidden warnings!

She felt for her sandals and flung back the curtains. This terrible muddle was not entirely her fault, it just felt that way!

At that moment Charlie came back, flushed and happy from the pool. She whirled round, clutching at her last pathetic straw of hope.

'Charlie, how can you be so sure Sarah is Brent's wife?' she asked him baldly. 'She might just share his house.'

He gaped in astonishment at her, but his answer was easy. 'Well, she signs her pictures Sarah Nicholson, and she wears a wedding ring. I always notice things like that now, ever since that time you explained to me about how you weren't married and you didn't wear a ring.'

'I see—I must just——'

She left him staring after her as she dashed, furious, along the path to the main building of the lodge. Brent must have seen her because he ambushed her outside the bar, his hand catching her arm. 'Kate!'

His fingers hurt. She tore herself free. 'Let me go.' She looked up into his face and her treacherous body quivered instantly with longing. But he was not the man she thought he was, and cold anger had damped down the fires of her love enough for her resolve to be unmoving.

'I was right from the start,' he grated. 'I knew you would regret what happened.'

'Of course I would—just the minute I knew the full truth about you and your double-dealing! Now leave me alone.' She gave him the full benefit of the cold stare she had perfected over the years, and had the bitter satisfaction of seeing him step back, confusion and anger fighting for supremacy in his face.

'What the hell are you talking about?'

'Don't pretend you don't know. How could you be so low? Now, excuse me, please!'

He stepped aside because the tone in her voice brooked no arguments. She hated that voice that had come back to her, the brittle, barking tone that had guarded her isolation all these years. No doubt it would be the voice of a lonely and bitter old woman. Even as she spoke she felt her muscles tense throughout her body. The relaxation of love had fled from her, and she stalked stiffly and unhappily away in search of Sandy.

With her logical mind she knew it was unfair to blame Sandy so much. It was Brent who had been so treacherous, and she who had allowed herself to go so readily into his bed. But what could you expect of men except lies and deceit? While Sandy was a woman, her friend, and should have been on her side. She could have told her the truth and stopped her from making such a fool of herself!

Sandy was where she thought she would be, checking over the tables for supper.

'Kate——' The steely look she encountered made Sandy exclaim in surprise.

'Why didn't you tell me Brent was married!'

'Married?' Sandy blinked twice. 'But he isn't. At least, as far as I know—I can't vouch for his early years, down south.'

'What about Sarah? Sarah Nicholson?'

'Oh, I see.' Sandy sank down at the table. 'Of course. Charlie. Oh, gosh, what a muddle.'

'Why didn't you tell me about her?' she challenged again.

'I did try. I warned you he wasn't the faithful type. Perhaps I should have said more, but I don't think you were in any mood to hear what I was saying.'

'You could have spelt it out a bit more clearly! Then I wouldn't have made such a damn fool of myself.'

Sandy indicated she should sit down with her and reluctantly she pulled back a chair.

'Look,' Sandy leaned on her elbows across the half-laid table, 'this isn't an excuse, but I wouldn't have known what to say to you if I'd tried. Sarah's been with Brent for years, but no one really knows what their relationship is.' She took a breath. 'Years ago Sarah was married to Brent's older brother, Mark. Mark died in a sailing accident about five years ago and about a year after that Sarah moved in with Brent. That's all I know. They don't go around together very much, they're both very busy people, with their own friends and commitments. We see far more of Brent than we ever do of Sarah.'

'I see.'

But she didn't really. Brent might not be married,

but it was obvious he had an involved and sophisticated relationship back in Nairobi. A relationship bonded by a shared past and a common future, which one night in a hotel bedroom with her was barely going to disturb.

Last night she had had an illusion that she was reaching down into his very soul, knowing him as intimately as she knew herself. But now she realised she knew nothing about him, nothing at all. Not his address, the colour of his car, or whether he drank tea or coffee in the morning.

It was as if she had been seeing him in stark black and white, but Sandy's words had shown her that she knew nothing of all the many shades and colours of his life.

She held her head between her hands, wanting to cry but fighting the tears.

Sandy put a hand on her arm. 'Surely there can't be that much harm done, Kate? Once you're back in London it'll seem like a dream.'

She laughed bitterly. 'Or a nightmare.'

'Did Brent say nothing at all about Sarah?'

She shook her head, wiping her eyes swiftly with the back of her hand.

'No. Although I should have realised—he certainly went out of his way to point out there was no future in getting involved with him. I was stupid enough to think it was just because he preferred to travel solo. I never dreamt there was a little wife—or wife-substitute—tucked away at home.'

'Maybe you should ask Brent about her. It might be quite a different sort of relationship.'

'I don't think I want to know, whatever sort of relationship it is. Quite frankly all I want to do is rub out the last twenty-four hours, or at least pretend they never happened. I certainly don't want to see him, Sandy. Not ever again.'

CHAPTER ELEVEN

THE gods had obviously decided to be kind and hear her plea. She stared through the open door of the room in disbelief.

'Has Mr Nicholson left?'

'Yes, ma'am. He left this morning, first thing.' All the books and papers had vanished, the cupboards were empty and open and the maid was methodically smoothing crisp white sheets on to the bed.

All that remained of Brent was a waste-paper basket, put by the door to be emptied. She stared at it as if hypnotised, searching for some clue to his sudden disappearance.

The basket was brimming with balls of paper, crushed tight as if by an angry hand, and she could just make out the odd fragment of a word here and there. One seemed to begin 'Ka——' and impulsively she bent down to smooth it out but then she straightened again, aware of the maid's curious gaze on her back.

'Did he—will he be coming back?'

'Not this time, ma'am. He said to me, "I'll see you next year, Rosie".'

'Thank you. I'm sorry to have bothered you.'

The maid went back to her tasks, making the now anonymous room ready for the next safari visitor. Kate glanced briefly at the bed. It could have been any bed, anywhere. What had happened there between her and Brent had been banished to the past for ever by Brent's decampment and the maid's efficient ministrations.

She turned and walked slowly away, seeking solitude among the trees and shrubs of the grounds.

This was the worst blow of all. In the night her anger had gradually abated. Brent had not been honest with her, he had told her nothing about his life with Sarah, but she began to concede that that was not quite the same as being married.

He had not deserved the anger she had flung at him, and at some point in the lonely small hours she had resolved to make her apologies.

But by the morning this resolve had flared into a burning need to see him again. She was like a woman possessed. She no longer cared about Sarah, or about his duplicity. She felt she would not have cared if he had bigamous marriages in every city in Africa, just as long as she could see him one more time, touch him, be held in his arms.

But instead of the warmth of his embrace she had found the awful emptiness of his room. There was no letter for her, not even a note under the door. He had just packed his things and gone, and when she saw Sandy and Mike later in the day the subject of his sudden departure was tactfully ignored.

After that the last days and hours dragged interminably, and even when they set out on their final game-viewing ride of the holiday, the indescribable beauty of the golden bush failed to move her.

'MMBA,' said Mike, as they crested a rise and saw the river plains stretching to the horizon. 'Miles and

Miles of Bloody Africa. You'll miss this when you're back in grimy old London.'

'Oh.' Charlie groaned. 'Why can't we live here, Mum?'

'What? Right here? In a tent? Living on zebra steaks?' She tried to make a joke, but her voice was brittle. She saw Mike glance up at her in his driving-mirror, his eyes anxious, and she guessed Sandy had told him of their sharp exchange yesterday morning.

She turned her head away and stared out at the tawny grassland, studded with flat-topped acacias, and dotted here and there with browsing game. The sun was almost gone, and with its departure came such a melancholy that if she had been a dog she would have put up her head and howled.

She longed to leave. The entrancing majesty of Africa had been reduced to the empty beauty of a chocolate-box painting by Brent's departure, and she felt like a dead woman inside, unable to respond to the life and colour around her.

Yet the next day, when they found themselves back at Nairobi's huge modern airport, the boom and bustle made her want to shriek with fright.

Two weeks among the quiet, slow rhythms of the bush had made them unfit for the modern world. Charlie clung to her side as they edged in a shuffling queue towards the check-in desk, and the garish colours of the magazines on the bookstall made her head pound.

Irrationally she found herself craning around, looking in every direction for the sight of Brent striding towards them.

She still could not believe what had happened, that he had really just gone without a word. There had to be a reason for it. She was sure he was not the kind of man to cut and run just because the going got difficult. Any moment he would come out of the crowd to find her, catch her up in his arms, and explain away the nightmare of his abrupt departure.

But then hadn't she been equally sure he was an honest and honourable man, and hadn't events proved just how flawed her judgement could be?

She had to face it, she knew nothing about him, and if her head had been turned by a chance encounter out in the romantic wilds she had only herself to blame for the painful consequences.

Yet her heart refused to be ruled by her head. When she caught sight of a dark-haired man elbowing his way towards them, her heart leapt into her mouth. But it was not Brent, but an older, thick-set man, who rudely pushed on past them to the front of the queue. Then someone caught at her arm and her heart hammered fit to burst, but it was only an airline clerk returning her dropped newspaper.

With leaden heart she handed over their tickets and saw their suitcases swallowed into the maw of the automatic luggage system. There was only a minute or two now before they would go through the departure gates and Africa, and with it Brent, would be behind them for ever.

'I don't want to go home, Mum,' Charlie said miserably.

'Neither do I.' She tried to pull herself together. 'Still,' she added with forced cheerfulness, 'I've got some change left, let's go and spend it. You'd look lovely in one of those hats with the zebra-skin band round.'

The hat now hung above Charlie's bed, slowly gathering a grey fur of dust as the constant stream of lorries rumbling along the main road near the flat kicked up a fug of grit and grime. Sometimes in the mornings, heading for work, Kate felt as if she could hardly breathe. The air was like soup, and everywhere she looked there were buildings and more buildings.

It was even worse in Oxford Street, where crowds perpetually swarmed up and down the pavements, and thr revolving doors of the store were never still as people pushed their way in and out.

It had been two weeks since they had got back, but she had found it impossible to adjust. She seemed to have lost all interest in the papers that piled up on her desk, and sat in near-silence through the meetings that punctuated her day. While people around her discussed 'kitchen events' and 'lighting weeks', she thought of the taunting, perceptive way Brent had rested his brown eyes on her, and how in the darkness of the African night she had spilled secrets to him that she had told no one before.

Night times were the worst, though, when her memories were hot and urgent, so overwhelming that she had to throw back the duvet and pace the room, wishing she smoked to calm her nerves.

Yet day by day she could see Charlie's tan fading before her eyes, and she knew she had to find a way of consigning all that had happened to the past, or she would end up a mad woman.

If only she and Brent had said their goodbyes, she thought. That way, at least, a line would have been drawn under the whole episode, and she would now be able to pack it away into a mental box labelled 'Momentary Madness', or 'Moment of Weakness', or whatever, and get on with her life.

But everything about their brief affair was unfinished. There were apologies unspoken as well as farewells unsaid. It felt, absurdly, as if Brent were still in her life, and every day she found herself looking for a letter from him, even though she knew it would be impossible since he had not the faintest idea—and no doubt not the slightest interest in—where she lived.

One lunch time, after a particularly mind-numbing series of meetings on window displays for the coming autumn, she stepped out of the store for a breath of air. All her colleagues were heading for a wine bar in Soho, but she had no stomach either for food or drink, or for office gossip.

'Excuse me. Please.'

The words came out with crisp exasperation. In summer visitors to London ambled along the pavements at a snail's pace, quite heedless of people going about their normal business.

She did not look at the man, only a blur of dark suit and white shirt that blocked her way. But the shape standing in her path did not seem to be making even a token effort to step aside on the crowded pavement. She looked up.

'No, I'm sorry. This time I don't plan to be elbowed aside quite so readily.'

The face sharpened slowly into the features that haunted her brain—those eyes, the nose, the sensual mouth.

'You—it can't be.'

She felt lost. The flow of people parted around them like the sea round an island and joined up again on the other side. This couldn't be Brent, not here. Not in London. Not in an immaculate suit and silk tie.

The dazzling white of his shirt made his tan look deeper, his eyes more penetrating. She found she was putting out a hand to feel if he were real. As she did so his fingers trapped hers. No skin had felt more real to her and the shock made her pull her hand back as if burnt.

'I was on my way to announce myself to your secretary when you came out. For a moment I wondered if it was you, you look so different. All that make-up, that smart suit—you hardly look real.'

It wasn't a compliment. 'I always look like this for work,' she snapped, nerves jumping.

'I preferred my African queen, in her jeans and her bush shirt.'

'Holidays don't go on for ever.'

Already her suspicious brain had worked out a reason for his being here. No doubt some business had brought him to London, and he had decided to see if she was in the market for continuing their casual affair. Maybe it could even become a regular arrangement, a girlfriend on tap in London, for whenever such an item might come in handy.

'Will you have lunch with me?'

'What are you doing here?' She ignored his question.

'I had to be in London on business, and I needed to see you.' So her first guess was right.

She thought of the empty room at the lodge, and all the hurt of his abrupt departure. He hadn't needed to see her then, and whatever he had come to say had obviously been able to await his convenience.

'I'm really very busy.'

'I see.'

His eyes searched hers, looking for the truth behind her words. 'I haven't got much time. Just today. I'm flying on to New York this evening. Kate,' he said forcefully. 'There are things we've got to sort out. Too much was left in the air.'

'Whose fault was that,' she said bitterly.

'I don't remember your being in much of a mood for rational discussion.' His eyes were so dark they were almost black, all their tawny lights banished, and his tone was as bitter as hers.

The crowds were jostling them, back and forth. 'Look,' he said with exasperation. 'At least have a drink with me, a cup of coffee even. I can't stand this.'

'All right,' she said reluctantly.

She indicated a café in a side street, an uninviting venue with dying rubber plants in its steamed-up windows. The only two seats left were at a small formica-topped table, next to two office girls who looked Brent appreciatively up and down.

Under the tiny table their knees touched as they took their seats. His closeness was unbearable, and she had to set down her cup because her hand was suddenly shaking so much. Yet it was not the Brent she remembered. This man was as besuited stranger.

'You thought I was married, didn't you? Charlie told you about Sarah and you put two and two together and made six.'

'There didn't seem to be any other explanation. I found out later it wasn't like that. Even so——'

He cut in angrily, 'Just because we share a roof doesn't necessarily mean we share a bed.'

The two girls next to them looked at him with undisguised interest. He quelled them with such a look that they drank down their tea and scrambled for their coats. When his eyes went back to her they held the same scathing displeasure.

'What are you doing here?' she burst out, unable to contain herself any longer. 'You were the one who kept saying there was no future for us, that I wasn't to expect anything from you. You vanish without a word, then turn up on my doorstep hundreds of miles away. Tell me what I'm meant to think! After all, you always have all the answers! But if you just want to establish a port of call in London, then you can save your efforts.'

'I'm not short of those, if I'm interested,' he said, succinctly. 'Which I'm not.'

'Then why?'

He scoured her face, and she could see herself through his eyes, her face painted and shaded like a sculpture, her shoulder-pads as hard as armour, her eyes glaring and cold. She shifted in her chair, uneasy and defensive.

'I needed to talk to you.'

He spread his hands on the table, the lean, supple fingers she remembered so well. She looked up at him. If she had been a stranger to him, then he might have been a different person from the laconic, teasing man she remembered loping so easily through the bush. His hair was tamed, his face set, and the dark suit rendered him as anonymous as any of the millions of executives who walked the pavements of the city.

The only thing unchanged was the quivering tension that charged the air between them, so tangible it could have been cut with a knife.

The scene felt unreal. Brent had been in her thoughts night and day, but his sudden appearance here, in her world, was too startling to cope with. Especially when the man sitting in front of her seemed so different from her memories.

'What can we possibly have to talk about?'

'Excuse me please, lady, gentleman, but if you are not going to eat, we need your seats.' A waiter had appeared at their side, scribbling a bill. 'I'm sorry, but it is lunch time. You can see the people queueing.'

'We'll eat,' Brent snapped. 'Anything.'

'No! I have to go.' She started up, suddenly unable to bear it any longer. 'I've got a meeting at two.'

The waiter was already ushering four people towards their table, and in the crush and confusion she began to push her way to the door. Behind her she heard Brent swear roundly. He followed her out.

'This is impossible.'

'Of course it is! What did you expect! If you'd wanted to talk to me so badly you could have done it before you left the lodge. If you're at all interested, I came to offer you my apology, only to find you'd gone without a word.'

'There were reasons for that. Good reasons.'

'I dare say, but they're nothing to me. It's all over now.'

'Kate, for goodness' sake!'

'Look,' she rounded on him, 'you turn up out of the blue——'

'Only because I knew that if I contacted you, you'd refuse to meet me.'

'Yes! Yes, I would! And I would have been right!'

'Kate!' He caught her arm. 'Don't do this to yourself——'

She pulled her arm free. 'Leave me alone! Just leave me alone!' she cried and turning, dived away into the anonymous crowd.

It took half an hour for the shaking to subside, and another ten minutes to mask the signs of crying on her face. People looked up curiously as she entered late to the meeting, and she knew they were wondering what had happened to her of late, that she should be doing her job so poorly.

She knew what had happened, she thought miserably, as she bent her head and drew convoluted doodles on her folder. Brent had happened. She loved him so much she hardly knew where to put herself. But when he had appeared in front of her, her dreams made flesh, she had run from him like a scalded cat.

It was because she was scared, she thought. No, not scared, utterly and completely terrified. She could not bear the pain and hurt of loving a man who did not love her, the hopes that came to nothing, the ultimate rejection. She had spent years building her defences against just such things and now they were under siege and she needed every last ounce of energy to defend them.

Only circumstances had made it possible, she reflected, the rushed and uneasy meeting among the jostling crowds, so different from the quiet intimacy they had known before. She allowed herself to close her eyes and think, swiftly and searingly, of the blue skies and open plains of Africa, and Brent's arms around her in the velvet night.

What had he come to say to her? Whatever it was, it would not, could not have been the words she longed to hear. And if she could not live with him, then she knew she had to live without him. Anything less than that, any temporary liaison or uneasy compromise, would sap away the foundations on which she had built her life, until she was as helpless and weak as the child she had been ten years ago.

She went back to her office. Her secretary looked up.

'The tickets have come. The man from the travel office is waiting I guess you have to sign for them.'

'What tickets? What man?'

'I don't know. I assumed you were off abroad again, and hadn't remembered to tell me. You've been a bit vague of late.'

'I know,' she snapped, 'but not that vague. I'm not going anywhere. There must be a mistake.'

She strode into her office. 'I think you must have the wrong——'

Brent turned from the window.

'You!'

'Me.' He crooked his mouth at her. 'Again.' And

he was no longer a stranger but the same man she had seen on the balcony, on that first magic morning in Africa, the man she now loved so helplessly. She put her hand to her desk to steady herself.

He was holding a brightly coloured folder, which he set down before her.

'What's that?'

'Airline tickets.'

'Airline tickets! Are you crazy?'

'Maybe. It depends on your definition of the word.'

She viewed them suspiciously.

'They don't bite.'

'What are they for?'

'You and Charlie. First-class returns to Nairobi. Open-dated.'

'I must be stupid. I don't follow you.'

His face was set again, and his voice hard, but she saw his hand stray to touch the bracelet of his watch and knew instinctively he was as on edge as she was.

'Look,' he said rapidly, 'there's no catch, I promise you. I've got to talk to you, Kate, we've got to spend some time together.' He gestured around. 'I can't do it here, not when there's so little time, and you're as jumpy as a cat, and you seem like a stranger to me anyway behind that mask of make-up. The tickets are paid for, you can come any time you like, leave any time you choose to.'

'I still don't understand. What's the point?'

He crossed the room and caught her hands tight in his. It was the first lengthy contact since they had met, and her body leapt up to his. His eyes were insistent.

'Kate, I'm asking you to do the very thing you find

impossible, the hardest thing anyone can ever ask you to do. I'm asking you to trust me. Please.'

She felt the power of his will, bending hers, and forced herself to remember again the betrayal of that stripped and empty room.

'Please,' he said again, through clenched teeth, as if he would drive the doubt from her eyes by sheer force. 'I won't hurt you. Not again. I promise.'

The doubt was still in her eyes as she looked at him, but deep inside her she felt something move and shift. It was like ice cracking before a thaw, or the first weak sunshine of spring. But she did not trust that feeling, did not trust Brent, did not trust herself.

His fingers still held hers.

'Will you come?'

'I can't just leave work again, not so soon. And Charlie's at school.'

'You can easily sort all that out, if you want to.'

She shook her head. 'I don't know——' She knew if he stayed another moment he would make her say yes. Gradually she realised that her phone had been buzzing for some minutes. 'You'll have to go. I've got someone coming to see me.'

He dropped her hands and picked up the tickets. 'Take these,' he commanded. She slowly took them. 'My address and telephone number are in there. I will be back in Nairobi on Thursday. If you decide to come, let me know.'

'And if I don't?'

He looked at her for the longest moment in history, and she knew he wanted to say, 'You will,' but he restrained himself. Instead he shrugged. 'Then I guess you just tear them up, and throw them in the bin.'

CHAPTER TWELVE

IN THE end it was Charlie who made the decision for her.

She told him nothing of Brent's reappearance, or his astonishing offer. Instead she watched him grow bored and listless, spending his time in the flat watching television, or playing desultory games of football with his friends on the scuffed patch of grass at the end of the road. She hated his being out on the streets while she was at work, but she hated even more the thought of his being cooped up indoors all the time.

One day she brought their holiday photos back from the developers and when Charlie's homework was finished they spread them out across the table.

It was like opening up the tiny room to sunlight and air. There were the elephants they had watched at the waterhole, on the first morning game-ride, with Brent. There were Adam and Joe in the swimming-pool, and Mike and Sandy smiling over dinner. There were zebras and giraffes and buffalo, all steeped in the glorious sun-drenched colours of the bush.

And there was Brent, in a photo Charlie must have taken because it leapt up at her, quite unexpected, from the pile.

'It seems as if it never happened,' said Charlie, scrutinising one picture, then another. 'It's like a dream, or something on television.'

'That rhino that charged you wasn't a dream.'

'No.' He grinned at the memory.

'Weren't you scared?'

'Only afterwards, when I thought about what might have happened. It must have been worse for you, watching it all happen.'

There wasn't really time to take it all in. Brent moved so fast.' She blushed as she said his name.

'I wish we could go back. Could we, Mum, next year?'

'I'm—not sure.' She packed the photographs away. 'We'll have to see. Come on, it's bedtime.'

In bed Charlie repeated his plea. 'I'd rather go there than anywhere in the world. When I grow up I'm going to live there. Adam and Joe are going to start a safari company, and I'm going to help them.'

She laughed, kissing him. 'It sounds wonderful. I'll be one of your first clients.'

He looked at her witheringly. 'No, you won't,' he said with the ruthless honesty of the young. 'You'll be too old by then. You won't want adventures any more.'

She looked at him, stunned. 'Is that what you really think?'

'Well——' He quailed a bit before her look. 'I don't know.' He looked suddenly angry and downcast. 'Actually I don't think we'll ever go back there, not ever!' he burst out. 'We'll probably stay in this horrid old flat till we die!'

His outburst shook her, she hadn't known he felt that way, and once he was mollified and tucked up she paced the living-room restlessly. Then she sat down and took out Brent's photograph.

He was leaning against the Land Rover, one foot bent up against the door, his jeans stretched tight over muscled thighs, his shirt undone carelessly, almost to the waist. He had a beer in one hand and his hat in the other and he was laughing at the camera.

How she loved that wicked expression, the one that deepened the smile-lines at the corners of his eyes and set off the taunting curve of his mouth. She looked at the gleam of his teeth and the brown column of his throat and ached into the depths of herself to see him again.

'Trust me,' he had said, but she had forgotten how to trust. And with Charlie to think of, taking any sort of risks, let alone flying off half-way round the world, seemed quite out of the question.

But Charlie wasn't happy; he had made that quite plain tonight.

Her thoughts went round in circles, tighter and tighter, around the same intractable problem. If they stayed as they were then—what? She would grow older, more bitter, more lonely, while Charlie's boredom and listlessness could quickly harden into a more dangerous adolescent resentment.

On the other hand, if they went to Kenya, if it worked out——

She hardly dared let herself think what 'it' might be. Brent had made no promises, offered no declarations. But looking again at the photograph, she knew that there was no choice. She had to see Brent again, she had to take a chance, risk everything in the hope, however slender, that she might get everything back.

The next evening she told Charlie.

'Next week, really? Wow!' He whooped and jumped about the flat. 'Where are we going? Are you going to marry Brent? That would be great!'

'Hold on, hold on.'

'I knew he was crazy about you. Everyone did. It was the way he looked at you, especially in your bikini.'

She swiped at him gently with a cushion. 'Little boys should be seen and not heard. Especially on this trip. I don't want a word out of you, do you hear? And you can forget marriage. Whatever Brent has in mind, it certainly isn't that.'

Yet she could not stop her heart singing with excitement at the thought of seeing him again, and although she felt acutely nervous about her decision, she knew also somewhere deep down that there had only ever been an illusion of choice.

That did not stop her feeling almost speechless with nerves by the time they alighted at Nairobi. Then there was a delay getting the baggage off the plane, and by the time they finally came out of the Arrivals Hall, her palms were damp with sweat and her mouth was dry.

Brent was there, though, the old, familiar Brent, in jeans and a khaki shirt, a jacket slung over one shoulder. She went instantly towards him but then she faltered, her nerve deserting her. She stopped and set down her bag. Charlie hung behind her. Brent looked at her, and she saw from the way his hand strayed to his watch that he was as nervous as she.

'You came. Even after your message I wasn't sure. I thought you might change your mind at the last moment.'

She shook her head. 'You should know I don't do that.'

Her eyes went to his, anxious, still uneasy. If only they could have touched, she thought, if only they could have embraced and kissed. But there was too much uncertainty in the air, too many unanswered questions, for that reassurance to be available.

He reached for her case, and greeted Charlie warmly.

'Hello, tiger, have I got a surprise for you.'

'What's that?' His boy's eyes were wide.

'Wait and see. Let me have a private word with your Mum first.'

He drew her aside, speaking briskly and rapidly. 'Listen, Sandy and Mike are in town. Adam and Joe have got the weekend off school. They're all at my house. If you're willing, I'd like to leave Charlie with them. There's something I want to show you.'

'What's that?'

'My farm.'

'Oh!'

'I'm not pushing Charlie out, believe me, Kate, but we need—I need some time with you alone. And he'll be in good hands.'

'Does Sandy know?'

He grinned, almost sheepish. 'This isn't just chance. It all took a certain amount of arranging.'

'Well——' She hesitated. 'I know Charlie will be thrilled to bits. Why don't you tell him?' Things were out of her hands, she could see that. Maybe they had been from the moment she and Brent had met. She had been fighting it tooth and nail, but now she gave up the struggle and the relief was enormous.

From that moment on, Brent was in charge. He shepherded them outside to a glossy black Land Cruiser, stowed their baggage, and drove to a house on the outskirts of the city.

Tactfully he suggested it might be best if they started straight away on the long journey, and she was glad to be spared Mike and Sandy's undoubted curiosity. From her seat she could see a low, white house and luxuriant gardens with shrubs and flowers, but it was scarcely a minute before Brent came back and started the engine.

'Look.' His eyes went over her face and she trembled, acutely aware of their new intimacy. 'It's a good few hours' drive from here, and you must be tired. Why don't you just relax and enjoy the journey, and we'll talk later.'

She nodded slowly, relieved at his words. 'Is Charlie all right?'

'On top form. Mike was planning to take them all swimming. With his contacts he has access to all the best hotels.' He looked at her again, his arms resting lightly on the wheel. 'You can leave him with an easy mind, I promise you. This time is for you, for us, and no one else. You're in good hands, I'll look after you and get you safely back to him. And meanwhile you can relax for once, and leave all your worries and cares behind. Enjoy the drive,' he commanded, 'and don't think about anything until you have to.'

He drove fast and skilfully away from the city, and the high-rise towers which dominated the horizon, down the coast road and then off towards the south and the Tanzanian border.

To her surprise she found she was enjoying herself. His quiet words had been like balm to her troubled spirit. She had never been looked after by anyone since she was a girl, and the feeling of letting go was a luxurious one.

After a time, though, the long, hot journey took its toll of her and she found her head growing heavy and her eyes closing.

She awoke to Brent's hand gently shaking her shoulder.

'Look. Kilimanjaro. I didn't want you to miss it.'

The snow-topped mountain rose like a vision from the blue heat-haze that thickened the horizon.

'It looks unreal, like a Japanese painting.'

'You can see it from the farm as well, only from a slightly different angle.'

She struggled upright and saw they were beginning to climb, out of the dry plains into lusher, greener hills.

'We're only about thirty miles away now, but the road gets much slower from here on. When the rains come it sometimes disappears altogether.'

'What happens then? Is the farm cut off?'

'It can be. There's a landing-strip on the farm, and a couple of my neighbours have their own aircraft, so essential supplies usually get through. And the farm is pretty self-sufficient, so there's never a serious problem.'

She looked at him. 'Why are you bringing me here?'

Brent looked across at her. 'I thought we agreed no talking till later. Apart from anything else, I need to concentrate from here on or we'll end up with a broken axle.' She sighed and looked out of the window, forcing herself to think of nothing except the scenery before her eyes until they arrived.

'This is the start of my land,' Brent said, as they crossed a small bridge. 'It goes to that rise over there, and as far as you can see in the other direction.'

She looked around with fresh interest, especially when he swung the jeep off the main track on to a narrower one that wound up the side of a slope to a low white farmhouse.

'Here.' He helped her down. She looked around. The house seemed unremarkable, a little run down, but he led her immediately through to the far side where a wide, creeper-shaded terrace ran the entire length of the building, opening on to a sloping terraced garden and a stunning view of blue hills ranging up to the distant peak of Kilimanjaro. On the veranda were tables and chairs, books and newspapers, even a hammock slung from the roof. She could see at once that this was the heart of the home, the place where drinks and meals were taken, and work done.

'I'll put your bag in your room and rustle up some tea,' said Brent, vanishing and leaving her alone. She paced about, feeling the peace and the silence after the long, lurching journey, and suddenly the memory came back to her of Sandy sitting on the veranda of her house in the game-park, darning Mike's sweater, while the cicadas sang up out of the dark.

How she had envied her that night, never dreaming

that such a life might be offered to her.

'Here.' Brent set down a tray. 'I'm only just getting organised here. The house hasn't been properly lived in for years. There's only a skeleton staff at the moment. Anny, the wife of my manager, has been acting as housekeeper, but she's away at the moment. Her eldest daughter has just had a baby, and she's gone off to the family village to do her grandmotherly duties.'

They sat drinking tea as dusk began to thicken the air. Brent said, 'This is an old planter's house. Built in the 1930s. It's as solid as——' he grinned wryly '—a house. The farm has some good land, but it could do much better than it has. It needs more trees, for one thing. Too much topsoil gets washed off in the rainy season. I also want to try and encourage some community projects among the farm workers' wives—it's the women who really run things in Africa, which is not a fact the Western aid agencies always appreciate.' He glanced up and saw her face. 'I'm sorry, you're tired. You don't want to listen to me giving a lecture.'

'It's not that. Only, I don't know what I'm doing here.'

He put up a restraining hand. 'Let me show you your room first. You can have a wash, change. Then we'll have the whole evening.'

He showed her to the unpretentious bedroom, apologising for the old-fashioned furniture. 'The whole place needs sorting out. I haven't had the time till now. I thought we'd eat about eight. It won't be very grand, just a sort of picnic.'

'Brent!'

The waiting was beginning to take its toll on her nerves.

He caught her shoulders, looking down into her eyes and the scent of his body, mingled with the dust and tiredness of the long drive, made her want to wrap her arms around him and lie down with him, somewhere safe and quiet, where there would be no difficult questions nor unacceptable answers.

'Rest a little,' he commanded. 'You need it.'

But rest was the last thing on her mind. Slowly she showered and changed, stepping into a cream linen dress whose long, fluid lines emphasised her tall slenderness. She wanted to make herself beautiful, but not painted and powdered like the woman she had left so far behind in London, and tension made her unusually indecisive. Eventually she compromised with a simple rope of pearls, a touch of mascara and only the lightest slick of lipstick.

Then there was nothing else to delay her, and although it was barely past seven she felt driven to go out.

On the veranda oil lamps had been lit, and some scented vapour was burning to deter the insects. A bottle was cooling in an ice bucket. She walked to the low wall, where steps led down to the lawn and the untamed garden. In her mind's eye she conjured up flowers in the weed-choked beds, and nursed the lawn back to luxuriant greenness.

Darkness covered the view but she knew that beyond the hidden hills lay thousands of miles of Africa. Somewhere far to the east lay the Indian

Ocean, and to the west, far off, the hot plains of the Serengeti.

What was it Mike had called it? MMBA. Miles and Miles of Bloody Africa. She took a deep breath of the cool night air. In the morning, she knew for certain, every leaf and flower and blade of grass would shine in the clear morning air as if it had been fresh-minted in the night.

It was so strange, the feeling she had. Away on every side of her stretched unknown horizons, yet she felt more at home here than she had ever felt in the noisy hustle of London.

There was a slight sound behind her and she turned just as Brent stepped through the doorway. He, too, had showered and changed. In the shadows, in dark trousers and a cream shirt, he looked taller, broader, more handsome than she had ever seen him.

He stopped as he caught sight of her, luminous as a moth in the soft light, her eyes huge and wary. Then he came to her and her mouth grew dry from the look in his eyes.

'Kate,' he said as he reached for her, and without pause she went into his arms. 'Oh, Kate.' He kissed her hair, pushed it back to kiss the softness of her neck, then found her lips and kissed her so deeply she felt she was drowning in him, and all he meant to her. It was the kiss she had dreamed of, night and day, since the last time she had been in his arms, but nothing in her fantasies had conjured up the passionate intensity of this moment.

'I want——' he began, drawing back to stroke her cheek. Then he crooked his mouth shakily and put himself from her. 'It's obvious. You know what I want.'

'No I don't. At least——' she smiled hesitantly '—not beyond——'

'You look more beautiful than I've ever seen you. I don't know how I'm going to keep my hands off you.' He pushed his hand through his hair, distracted, then he turned. 'Let me get you a drink, and then I'll put myself firmly on the other side of the table. That way I might, just might be able to do the talking I promised you.'

He poured wine and his voice hardened. 'You certainly look a hundred times more yourself than you did in London. There I was, carrying this crystal-clear image of you in my head, and suddenly there was this painted mannequin in front of me.' He turned to hand her a glass. 'I don't mind telling you, I began to wonder if I was quite right in the head.'

'I told you, I have to look like that for my job. It just makes it easier, to look the way people expect. And it was exactly the same for me. It seemed so odd to see you there, in the middle of all those people. I hated how it was between us. One of the reasons I decided to use the tickets was to try and scrub out that memory.'

'One of them—what about the others? The other reasons.'

'Why did you give me them?' she parried hastily.

'I—there was so much that was unfinished between us. It seemed the only way it was ever going to get sorted out after the way you ran out on me in London. Look, come and sit down.'

She took a seat and he sat, as he had promised,

across the table.

'You won't know this, but I tried to catch you at the airport, before you left Kenya.' She looked up in astonishment. 'I left the lodge because there were things I had to sort out in Nairobi—I'll tell you about that in a minute—but I really did want to straighten things out between us before you left.'

'I rang your travel agent and got the time of your flight and started to drive to the airport. But there'd been a major pile-up on the road. A lorry had gone out of control, ploughed into a line of cars, had turned over and one caught on fire.' He glanced up at her. 'Driving in Africa is a bit like that at times.'

It was as if he was testing her reaction.

'So is driving on the M1,' she replied crisply.

'You can imagine the mess. The road was totally blocked in both directions for more than two hours. I waited about an hour, then I tried to get to a phone, but by the time I got through to anyone who could have stopped you, the plane was boarding.

'My language that morning was far from polite, I can tell you! I wanted to tear my hair out at the frustration. Then I thought about writing to you, or telephoning you, but I knew I had to go and see my publishers in London later in the month, so it seemed sensible to try and see you then.' He drained his glass and refilled it. 'With hindsight, I can see that was a lousy idea.'

'You should have warned me. If I'd known you were coming it wouldn't have been such a shock.'

'You wouldn't have seen me,' he said realistically. 'You might not remember exactly how you treated me at our last meeting, but I do. Every word is etched into my brain.'

She blushed. 'I had no right to say the things I said; I found that out later. In fact I came to apologise to you—that's when I discovered you were gone.'

The desolation, the betrayal of that empty room still had the power to hurt, and she tensed defensively against the memory.

'I tried to leave you a note, but for once words failed me.' He sighed. 'You thought I was married, didn't you? It's a mistake lots of people make when they hear Sarah's surname.'

'But you live together.' She held her breath, desperately hoping for a denial.

'Lived—and even that isn't quite accurate. Look.' One hand strayed to his watch-strap, to finger it abstractedly. He had such beautiful hands, she thought, irrelevantly. The strain between the two of them seemed to be making her mind fly in all directions. 'I suppose Sandy told you Sarah was my brother's wife? After the accident she wanted to move up to Nairobi, and she was so distressed it didn't seem a good idea for her to live alone, so I offered her a room in my flat.

'After a time she gradually got her strength back and began to paint again, and since we were both only there about half the time, sharing a flat seemed to work well enough. When Sarah decided she needed a studio, it seemed sensible to buy a house together.'

'You mean she never was your girlfriend?'

He paused, looking at her long and dark. 'The easy answer would be to say no, and leave it at that, but life is never quite that simple. I need to be honest with you, Kate. There was a time, about two years ago, when we got involved for a time. Sarah had mourned Mark as fully as she could, and she was obviously ready to move on to new relationships. I suppose I was simply there, and she knew me well, and we were close.'

He paused.

'And you?' she breathed.

He hesitated, seeking words. 'I'd always been attracted to her, and it began to seem inevitable that our relationship would change. But it just didn't work. We got on fine as two separate people, but as a couple we were a disaster—rows all the time. I saw the way things were going before she did, but gradually she, too, accepted it wasn't going to work.

'Luckily I had to go away, off on a long swing through Africa, and when I came back, she was just off on a painting scholarship to Canada, and by the time we were both back in Nairobi together six months had gone by and we were able to go back to how things had been before.' He looked up, his eyes suddenly piercing and direct. 'Sarah is very special to me; she always will be. We've been through a lot together. That's why I left the lodge when I did.'

She frowned. 'I don't understand.'

He stood up and paced the veranda. 'Kate, something happened for me, during that night we spent together. From the moment I first met you, you'd really got under my skin. The more I saw of you, the more time we spent together, the more obsessed I became. You were in my thoughts night and day.

'I'd never met a woman like you, so strong and independent, and yet so soft and hurt at the centre. I thought—I still think—you're the most beautiful, arresting woman I've ever met. You remind me of some nervous, haughty animal, forever ready to shy off at any hint of danger. You seemed so enigmatic, so unknowable. At first you were a challenge. I wanted to crack your defences, unravel your secrets. Then I simply wanted you so badly I hardly knew what to do with myself.'

He stopped, turning to look at her, and her heart knocked with longing for him.

'I never wanted to hurt you, you must believe that. I really didn't want to hurt you—Kate——' He turned, and his knuckles were white as he clenched his hands. 'This is the difficult bit. Even when we went back to my room together that night, when you were offering yourself to me, the very last thing on my mind was any sort of long-term relationship. I'd always been a free agent, doing what I wanted, when I wanted, and I saw no reason to change all that. I wanted you there, with me, in my bed, but on my terms only. I wanted to possess you, to purge my brain of you, and then I wanted to walk away as free as ever.

'It isn't very edifying, I'm afraid, but that's the truth of the matter, and to square my conscience, I insisted that you understood the terms.'

'You certainly succeeded on that count,' she said bitterly.

'But it didn't work,' he said. 'During those hours we spent together I realised we were at the start of something, not the end. I knew it wasn't enough, that we needed more than just that one night together.'

'Oh?'

She got up suddenly, shaking all over. All at once the pieces had fallen into place and she hated the pattern they made! How could she have been so foolish as to expect anything else?

'So that's what those tickets were for! An invitation back for a few more! Until you've had you fill of me.' She flung herself round to glare at him.

'Kate, for goodness' sake!'

Brent came to her, wrapping her round in an iron embrace. 'I'm not putting it very well,' he said hoarsely, 'but I can hardly think straight with you looking as beautiful and untouched as a piece of bone china—you fill up my head, my thoughts, until I can barely speak.'

Through her anger and despair she knew the feeling. His closeness and warmth, the breath on her cheek, the anticipation of his lips made her thoughts reel. She turned her head and pushed him away, as hard as she could. Then she began to run, heading for the safety of her room. She couldn't bear it, she just couldn't bear it! If she let him love her now, the later hurt would destroy her completely!

But her steps had led her the wrong way. She faltered at the end of the veranda.

'No. No.' Brent strode after her, pulling her roughly round to face him. 'Oh, no, you don't run out on me again!'

She saw his chest heaving.

'I don't understand,' he said harshly. 'Why did you

come back if the thought of spending more time with me so horrifies you?'

What could she say? I had this foolish hope—I thought you might love me, might even marry me?

'Because I was a fool,' she flung at him. 'Because I never seem to learn from my mistakes.'

'Everyone makes mistakes,' he blazed back. 'Only most people manage to put them behind them and get on with living. They don't bottle them all up inside and freeze off everyone who comes within striking distance!'

'Perhaps they should! Because in my experience every man I've ever come across is devious, untrustworthy and utterly selfish! And that includes you, Brent Nicholson!'

'Why me?' he said his eyes narrowing dangerously.

'Why—because you've brought me out here, all this way, just for what? To take off where we left off?'

His eyes seemed to taunt her cruelly. 'And why not? It seems a very good place.'

Abruptly he pulled her closer, hard against him, and crushed his lips down on hers, merciless in his pent-up passion. The embrace was short, savage and left them both gasping for breath. 'Don't you think?' he continued.

Then he kissed her again, still punishingly, and moved his hands to cup and fondle her breasts into quickening life. She lifted her face to his, all but lost in the sensations he was rousing, her anger seeping away into hopeless despair. She saw his eyes, intent, not smiling, his lips parted, a blaze of colour along his cheeks. His breath was uneven as he touched her.

I love you, she thought. How I love you! The thought came out as a muted cry of desire and despair.

She turned her head against his chest and said bitterly, 'If you want to make love to me, you can. You know that. You know you can do whatever you want with me.' She closed her eyes with pain and shame at her weakness.

His palms moved down her sides, the slenderness of her waist, to rest on the points of her hips.

'Is it what you want?' He was so close to her she could hear the rasp of his voice in his throat.

'Yes, now—but not later.'

'Why not later?'

She thought of the empty room at the lodge, the door flung wide.

'Because then you'll be gone. Maybe not tomorrow, but some time.'

'Trust me. Please, Kate. Let go. You don't have to be so full of fear.'

'You went before.'

'You mean from the lodge?'

'Yes.'

'I had to. There were things I wanted to say to you, but I had to speak to Sarah first.' Slowly her eyes lifted to his. 'Kate, I told you something happened to me that night we were together. A lot of things fell into place. I did a lot of hard thinking the next day and made some decisions that I needed to tell Sarah about. That's why I left for Nairobi. I wanted to tell her I was giving up my half of the house altogether. Before, I thought I might keep it on even when I moved out here, to the farm, but suddenly I knew I wanted to give it up, give up my old life altogether. I also needed to tell her I——' he paused, searching carefully for words '—had met someone who I hoped might share this life with me.'

Her eyes widened.

He went on, 'That might sound strange, but I felt she had a right to know. She's been close to me for so long, in different ways. I also knew she would tell me if she thought I was making a complete fool of myself.' He smiled slightly. 'She actually said she'd never seen me in such a state and she looked forward to meeting the woman responsible.'

Kate shook her head slowly. Her brain seemed to have stopped working.

'You mean, you want—me——?'

He looked at her anxiously.

'Perhaps it's madness to think it would work. You're used to a very different kind of life. That's why I wanted you to see the place.'

She looked at him. Her heart wanted to flower with flooding joy, but her distrustful head would not let it. Instead it mocked and taunted. He thinks you'll make a useful working partner, it said, and he fancies you in bed. But what about when he grows tired of you? What happens then? After all, he told you himself, he always grows bored with things in the end.

She shook her head. 'I don't know—I'd have to give up so much, my job—and Charlie, what would he do?'

'Charlie could go to school with Adam and Joe in the week, and come back at weekends. He'd love it. There would be no problem there. I don't know what to say about your job. You said you didn't like it very much, and if you need a challenge you only have to look around.'

'But if it didn't work?'

'It will,' he said firmly, pulling her closer. 'Kate, it will, it will. I know it.'

She felt her will being bent by his stronger one. 'How can you know it?' she said, and there was bitterness in her tone. He was asking her to give up everything for him. But what was he offering in return? He had said nothing of his feelings, never said that he loved her.

His eyes searched hers.

'Do you really have to ask me that question?'

'Yes. Yes, I do.'

His hands spread up to her shoulders, then up underneath her hair, cupping her head. 'I thought it was so obvious. Because I love you, Kate. Because I can't live without you. Because we have to drive to Nairobi tomorrow, and get married just as soon as possible, and you have to be my wife, my friend, my partner, my helpmeet, the mother of my children. Do I have to go on?'

His eyes were on hers, smiling down at her, but with an edge of apprehensive waiting that softened her watchful gaze. Slowly the full weight of his words sank in, washing away her doubts, and thawing the ice of her damaged heart.

'Oh, Brent, I love you too. I have done for so long.'

'Trust me, Kate. I'll never leave you again. I'll never let you down. And it will work between us, I give you my promise.'

Slowly her eyes searched the depths of his, and her lips rose to meet his kiss.

'I do,' she at last allowed herself to say. 'Oh, I do, Brent. I do trust you. I always will.'

Harlequin Presents

Coming Next Month

Available in January wherever paperback books are sold, or through Harlequin Reader Service:

In the U.S.
901 Fuhrmann Blvd.
P.O. Box 1397
Buffalo, N.Y. 14240-1397

In Canada
P.O. Box 603
Fort Erie, Ontario
L2A 5X3

ATTRACTIVE, SPACE SAVING BOOK RACK

Display your most prized novels on this handsome and sturdy book rack. The hand-rubbed walnut finish will blend into your library decor with quiet elegance, providing a practical organizer for your favorite hard-or soft-covered books.

Only $9.95

Approximately 16" x 8" when assembled

Assembles in seconds!

To order, rush your name, address and zip code, along with a check or money order for $10.70* ($9.95 plus 75¢ postage and handling) payable to *Harlequin Reader Service*:

Harlequin Reader Service
Book Rack Offer
901 Fuhrmann Blvd.
P.O. Box 1396
Buffalo, NY 14269-1396

Offer not available in Canada.

BKR-1A

*New York and Iowa residents add appropriate sales tax.

Step into a world of pulsing adventure, gripping emotion and lush sensuality with these evocative love stories penned by today's best-selling authors in the highest romantic tradition. Pursuing their passionate dreams against a backdrop of the past's most colorful and dramatic moments, our vibrant heroines and dashing heroes will make history come alive for you.

Watch for two new Harlequin Historicals each month, available wherever Harlequin books are sold. History was never so much fun—you won't want to miss a single moment!